MANDRAKE

BOOK 6 OF THE

POISON GARDEN

CONTENTS

Not Okay

We still weren't talking about it.

After Dan got the text announcing Alicia's pregnancy, and I threw up at the sight of a pan full of scrambled eggs, I went back to bed. Maybe this was all a dream. Or maybe it was an alternate reality, and I could get a do over. Not that I could, or even would, change things. I just needed time to catch my breath, and think.

Dan let me wallow in my feelings for about an hour, then he came to check on me. He sent Stuart in first, and let the pup gallop around the room for a few minutes before he joined us. For a moment, he stood in the doorway, his arms crossed over his chest and his stance wide. His dark hair was tousled and his brows were low, and I felt awful. While I'd been up here staring at the ceiling, he'd been downstairs all alone, worrying about me.

"Hi," I said.

"Hey." Stuart *wuffed* at him, so Dan picked him up and plopped him on the bed.

"Hey, Stuart." I scratched behind his ears, always up and at attention, although the left one tended to flop over. That made him extra adorable. "You keeping an eye on Dan?"

"He supervised as I cleaned up from breakfast, then he let me take him out," Dan said; soon after we brought the fluffy brown dog home, it became apparent that Stuart now ruled the house. We were all okay with that. "How are you feeling?"

"Better," I said, though I was still tired. However, the lack of eggs in close proximity to me meant I was no longer nauseous, and that was a definite improvement. "Sorry I got all dramatic earlier."

"It's all right. We just won't have eggs for a while." Dan sat next to me. I snuggled up against him, then Stuart decided to get in on the action and wedged himself between us. "Want to talk about it?"

"I... I just want to stay like this, for now."

Dan kissed my hair. "Sounds like a plan."

And so we sat, silently holding each other while the biggest elephant in the history of elephants sat in the room with us. After a few minutes of forced relaxation, my phone beeped.

"You gonna get that?" Dan asked, then his phone beeped, as well. "Might be a case."

"Might be." I grabbed my phone, and saw a text from Jill Sanders. She was one of Dan's closest friends from when he was on the police force. "Jill texted me."

"Me, too. She said there's something, and I quote, weird happening downtown."

"That's what she said to me, too," I said, then I replied.

Eli: How weird, and where downtown?

Jill: Very, and at the park next to City Hall.

Eli: We'll be there in ten.

"You sure you're up for it?" Dan asked. "I can go alone."

"I'll be fine," I replied, as I got out of bed and went in search of my boots. "Besides, if this is magical weirdness, you'll need me."

"All right, babe," Dan said, then he shooed Stuart off the bed and grabbed his coat. "Let's check out the latest nonsense."

Fifteen minutes later, Dan parked our SUV on Main Street. We saw the police cars congregated around the park entrance, then I spotted something far more interesting than a few cruisers with flashing lights. Even though it was still winter, there was a group of mandrake plants in full flower clustered around at the base of the lamppost.

"Here's the first something weird." I crouched down, and poked at the rosette of leaves. "I've never seen mandrakes in this park."

"And that's something you would have noticed?" Dan asked.

"Oh, yeah. As far as magical plants go, mandrake is herbal royalty." I straightened up, and saw another one of the plants farther inside the park. "There's more."

"Let's follow the trail," Dan said. "Gotta say, I'm almost used to plants asking you for help."

"Almost?"

"I'm holding a grudge against the mistletoe."

I grabbed Dan's hand, and we followed the mandrakes. They were scattered around the park, poking up through the snow and hiding behind benches and statues. The path wended behind City Hall, close to where the police had set up. While Dan went toward the officers to find Jill, I visually tracked the mandrakes to the base of an oak tree, then I remembered a certain bit of lore about these plants.

Mandrakes were said to sprout beneath a hanged man.

I looked up, and saw three bodies swaying from the upper branches. Pinned to the center body's torso was a sign that had "witch" scrawled across it in violent red letters.

"There you are," Jill said, as she and Dan joined me. "Like I was telling Dan, someone staged the execution of three supposed witches behind City Hall."

I looked at Jill, then back up at the bodies, then I bent over and puked.

"You okay?" Jill asked.

"No." I wiped my mouth, and looked up at the bodies. *Witch* bodies. If people were out here murdering witches, how could I bring a baby witch into the world? "I'm pretty far from okay."

While the medical examiner took pictures of the bodies, Dan and I went inside with Jill. She'd turned one of the ground floor offices into a staging area, and we watched her issue orders to a few uniformed officers. Speaking of which...

"I thought you were forensics," I said, when the three of us were finally alone. "When did you get promoted? Or demoted?"

"Neither of those events happened," she replied. "Chief specifically wanted to call you two in to consult on this case, and he thinks you'll only work with me. Therefore, I get to lead this investigation in all my forensics glory."

Dan grunted. "I take it Chief's still mad at me for not coming back to the force?"

"Oh, yeah." Jill shuffled through some papers on the desk. "He gave me a big speech about how you're a gifted detective and wasting your career chasing cheating spouses and suspected insurance fraud."

Dan scowled, and took a breath so he could tell Jill how he really felt. Before that could happen, I took his hand. "Tell Chief it's all my fault. I'm a wicked bad influence," I said. Dan squeezed my hand, and I felt his tension melt away. His ears stayed red, though.

"Yeah, Eli. You're wicked bad, all right." Jill handed me a sheet of paper that listed the few known facts about the case. "We know almost nothing about the victims as of yet. We're fairly certain they didn't work here in City Hall, though we haven't had time to interview everyone who works here." Jill bit her lip. "So. Are they witches?"

"No idea," I replied. "I could barely see their faces up there. What I can tell you is that historically, way more innocent mortals have been executed for witchcraft than actual witches."

"Interesting," Jill said. "Why would someone execute a mortal and stage it to look like a witch?"

I shrugged. "The usual reasons. Money, revenge, removing powerful women, stuff like that."

"Wait," Jill said. "What's that about removing powerful women?"

"When women have power, and men want to discredit them in order to steal their power, they cry witch," I replied. "Read up on the Salem trials, or any witch trials, for that matter. An awful lot of outspoken, powerful women—as in, women who made their own money, owned their own businesses, and did things their own way—ended up being accused. It's no different from how a weak man will call a strong woman bossy or a bitch, because he's jealous of her power."

Jill rubbed her eyes. "This is all rather timely, then, because the mayor is up for reelection. Running against him is Senator Stevens's sister, Lillian."

"I didn't know Barbara had a sister." Back when I first became a private investigator, I found a kidnapped girl named Abigail Stevens. The fact that I rescued her with help from a ghost was beside the point. Far more interesting was that Abby's mother was the legacy senator, Barbara Stevens. As politicians went, in this state, the Stevens family might as well be royalty.

"They're not close," Jill said. "Why, I don't know. But the senator has endorsed the mayor for reelection, and Lillian has retaliated by publicly dragging her family through the mud."

"That doesn't seem like an effective campaign strategy," I said.

"Maybe it is, maybe it isn't," Jill said. "What I do know is that we have two powerful women butting heads, there is a nasty political campaign culminating in an election in a few weeks, and now we have dead people hanging behind City Hall. Odds on all of this being connected?"

"I'd say the odds are good," Dan said. "How soon before we get some names?"

"Soon." Jill whipped out her phone. "Actually, now. They all had their wallets and identification on them."

"I guess that rules out robbery," I said, as Jill sent images of the victims' driver's licenses to my and Dan's phone. "I don't recognize any of these people," I said, as I swiped through the images.

"Me neither," Dan said. "We can ask a few people in the supernatural community and rule out them being known witches, at least."

"You also need to check out the ground beneath where they were hanging," I said. "There's mandrake scattered all over the park, which is weird for the time of year. Also, standard herbal lore says that mandrake grows beneath a hanged man."

"Which feeds into your theory that this murder is being set up to make people look like they're witches, when they're not," Jill said. "I'll have a team sweep the entire park, and let you know what we find. Thanks, guys."

"Any time," I said, then Dan and I left Jill in her makeshift office. It took us a while to leave the building, since every officer along the way had to stop Dan and say hi.

"Do you ever miss being on the police force?" I asked, when we'd finally gotten past all the well-wishers.

"I miss the idea of being on the force, but no, I don't miss being a cop," he replied. "I only joined because I needed a job with good insurance, and my brother, Carmelo, was already on the force. I was a bad fit for the job from the beginning."

I looped my arm with his, and leaned against him. "I think it was a great fit, since you being a cop is what led to us meeting."

Dan kissed the back of my hand. "When you put it that way, I agree." He spotted something on the ground near the bottom of the building's wide staircase. It was one of the mandrakes. "Look at this."

We bent down, and examined the plant. Now that I was looking at it up close, and saw the ring of disturbed earth around the base of the plant, it was obvious that it had been hastily stuck in the ground, and hadn't grown here naturally.

"The killer, or an accomplice, brought these plants here." I grabbed the mandrake's leaves, and pulled it straight up out of the ground. "I bet these plants haven't even been here for a full day."

"You mean to tell me that someone had the time to bring three bodies behind City Hall, string them up, and do some landscaping, and no one noticed anything?" Dan shook his head. "This was a complex operation."

"You think the victims were already dead when they were hung?"

"Makes sense. Living people would put up a hell of a fight, scream, the whole nine yards." Dan stood, and surveyed the courtyard. "There is a lot going on here."

"There is." I set my hand on my belly. *And we need to figure it out, before these lunatics come for our baby.*

PANCAKES

After Eli and I finished up at City Hall, we took our time walking back to the truck. We were halfway across the street when I saw crumbs of dirt falling out from Eli's coat.

"Did you take one of the mandrakes?" I asked.

"What makes you say that?" she countered. "Besides, it might want to talk to me."

"Eliza. You can't just grab evidence." Which she was very well aware of. "That all needs to be catalogued."

"I'm the Mistress of Seers, which means that all baneful herbs are under my jurisdiction," she said, which was a lame argument. However, I knew better than to go down this path with her, especially about one of her new plant friends.

We got to the truck, and I unlocked the doors. Eli popped the hatch and found a plastic bag to stash her contraband plant in. "I'll see if it wants to tell us anything later, after it's had a chance to perk up."

"Jill is going to know you took that, and she is going to be pissed." We got in the car, and I started the engine. "Where to now?"

"Not sure," she admitted. "I'm a bit hungry for pancakes."

I thought about the scrambled eggs incident from that morning, and decided not to mention it. Nothing in heaven or earth could make Eli talk before she was ready. "Want to hit the diner?"

A line formed between her eyebrows; I could imagine the thoughts swirling around her mind, wondering what kind of foods and smells she might encounter there. I was wondering that myself, since I didn't want her getting sick in public, or anywhere else for that matter.

"Actually, can we go to the grocery store?" she asked. "That way, we can make pancakes at home."

"You mean I can make you pancakes at home," I said, and she didn't dispute. Between the two of us, I was the better cook, and neither one of us minded one bit. Plan established, I drove to the nearest grocery store. Once we were there, Eli grabbed a cart and made a beeline straight toward the pancake mixes. I noticed that she got the kind that only needed water to come together, no eggs or other ingredients necessary. She earned some points for planning ahead.

"Why is the syrup in a different aisle?" she muttered, as we went in search of maple goodness. To my surprise, she ignored the pure syrups and went for a brand that was little more than flavored corn syrup. "Do we have butter at home?"

"I'll go grab some, just in case," I said, since I did not need her puking at the sight of milk. By the time I got back to her, she'd added granola bars, muffins, and chocolate chip cookies to the cart.

"I guess you are hungry," I said. "Do we need anything else?"

"I'm good. Oh, potting soil for the mandrake," she added.

We swung through the florist department and grabbed a bag of dirt, then we paid, and got out of there. While I loaded up the truck, Eli checked her phone.

"Get anything good?" I asked, as I slid behind the wheel.

"I was just checking for updates from Jill," she said, as she dropped her phone into her bag. "Although I guess it is too soon for her to know anything else."

"You never know," I said. "Everything can change in the blink of an eye."

"Tell me about it." Eli looked down at her stomach. "I mean, I figured this would happen eventually, but not now. Not so fast."

I paused with the key hovering over the ignition. Eli had not only acknowledged that she was pregnant, she sounded as if she was okay with it. As in, we were going to have a baby.

Holy shit, we're gonna have a baby.

I unfastened my seat belt. "Back seat."

Eli blinked. "What? Why?"

"If you're in a mood to talk, we're talking. Right here, right now."

"We can talk at home," she began, but I wasn't having any arguments.

"Oh, no." I got out of the front and went into the back, and continued, "Knowing our luck, we'll run into a herd of unicorns or get attacked by flying squirrels. We'll do this right here in the parking lot like the lunatics we are."

Eli gave me a look that told me she questioned my logic, then she climbed over the seat like an acrobat and sat beside me. "This is silly. I feel like we should make out or something."

"Maybe later." I moved so I was facing her, and set my hand on her knee. "So. You start."

"Why me?"

"You're the main character here. I just go along with your whims."

"I don't have whims," she said, then she studied her hands in her lap. "I think I've known about the baby for a while, but I didn't want to admit it to myself. Admitting it makes it real, you know what I mean?"

"Yeah." I tucked a piece of hair behind her ear. "How long have you known?"

"Remember the first time we went up to the Christmas tree farm, and we burnt the dendromancy basket right afterward? The smoke showed us a baby."

"I remember." She was referring to the farm up in Yorktown Heights, which was run by an ice demon with a grudge against my family. Like I said, our luck was crazy. "That was more than two months ago."

She nodded. "I know. When the smoke took on the shape of a baby, I figured that was because we would have one eventually, but the more I thought about it, the more I realized I was wrong. Those sorts of spells only work on the caster's present state. It must have just happened," she added. "I didn't feel any differently back then, but the magic knew. Magic always knows the truth, no matter how hard you try to hide it."

"Then you were pregnant back in December," I said, and she nodded. "How can you be sure? No offense, babe, but a smoky image of a baby isn't exactly hard evidence."

Eli looked up at me with her big, brown eyes, and said, "The holly."

I blew out a breath, and even though I'm an ex-cop with my feet firmly planted in the real world, I admitted that was a solid clue. Plants loved to talk to Eli, and when you added that to her incredible power levels, it meant she could manifest them based on her moods. The first time we slept together, she manifested acres of bleeding hearts, which was how she told me she loved me. In the hotel room in New York, we'd woken up to a bed full of holly, a plant which was known for influencing fertility.

"That's why you freaked out and jumped in the shower," I said, and she nodded. After I'd cleaned up the holly, I joined Eli in the shower. As we stood under the water, she told me her biggest fear was that she'd be an awful parent, like her mother was.

Frankly, that was bullshit, and I told her so. Eli was the most caring, compassionate person in the world, and I was lucky to call her my wife. At the time, she'd acted reassured, but now I wondered.

"Hey. Come here." I extended my arm, and Eli nestled herself against me. Holding her was, without a doubt, the best feeling in the world. "I love you, baby."

"I love you, too." She kissed my throat, and I had to remind myself we were in a public parking lot. "I'm sorry I didn't say anything sooner. I got the idea that if I ignored it, I wouldn't have to deal with it, and that was very much not right."

I chuckled at her wording, but what she said gave me pause. "You know, you don't have to do this. It's your choice, one hundred percent."

She looked up at me, her brows pinched together. "But... But if we don't have this baby, you'll be heartbroken."

I stroked her cheek. "The only thing that would break my heart is if I lost you."

Eli reached up and ruffled my hair; it was due for a cut, but she kept playing with it and I liked that, so I kept putting it off. "Good thing I'm not going anywhere. And... I want this. I want our baby."

"Yeah?" I asked, hardly believing this was my life.

"Yeah." She laid her head on my shoulder and her arm snaked around my waist. "Let's give this parenthood thing a go. It'll be fun, right? Wait, we should probably tell your mom."

"And your dad. And Tess. And about a million other people."

"See? All fun things." Eli grinned at me. "As much as I love snuggling with you, can we go home? It's kinda cold without the heat running, and my pancakes won't make themselves."

"Whatever you want, baby."

TAROT CARDS

As soon as we got home, I put the mandrake in a pot with fresh soil, gave it some water, and set it on the windowsill with the kitchen herbs. Hopefully that would revive it, and, after a day or so, the plant would tell me something about the murders. Once that was done, I ended up making the pancake batter, because Dan turned into Mr. Home Improvement.

"What are you doing?" I asked, when he made his third trip into the basement.

"I gotta make a list of what we need for the nursery," he said, as he hauled a toolbox out of the basement. "We'll need a bassinet, and a crib—"

"Isn't a bassinet just a small crib?" I asked. "Why do we need both?"

"It's for when the baby's smaller. Like an infant."

"Aren't all babies small?" I put the batter in the fridge to rest, then I went into the living room and opened my laptop.

"What are you doing?" Dan asked, as he walked by with even more tools. Apparently, he was going to chop down a tree and build a nursery from scratch. "Making a baby registry?"

"I'm researching recent murders, to see if our killer has a pattern." I glanced up. "Why would I need to register the baby? He won't even be here until September-ish."

"September?" Dan grinned. "That means we can have a big summer party to get ready. It will be the best baby shower Queens has ever seen!"

"We're going all the way to New York for a baby shower?"

"We can have two," he said, because my husband had clearly lost his mind. "One here, and one at Nonna's."

"You are out of control." I left him to his baby shower and nursery dreams, and returned to my research. There weren't any murder reports similar to what had happened in the park in the recent past, so I started looking into the three victims. When I entered the second victim's name, Colleen Bergquist, I found a video of her reading tarot cards in a booth at a farmers market.

"Dan, check this out." I angled my laptop around so we could watch the video together. Our victim was decked out in glittery scarves and stacked bangle bracelets like a fortune teller on a prime time sitcom.

"So she was a witch." Dan glanced at me. "Wasn't she?"

"Maybe. Tarot card reading is one of those gray areas where it's as much about skill as it is about magic. Mundane humans can definitely learn how to use tarot as well as any witch or seer with foresight, and some of them far surpass us. There are also tons of people out there who just pick up a deck and use it as a prop to con desperate people out of their money," I added.

"Which do you think she was?"

"Hard to tell from this video." I hit pause, and scrutinized her set up. The booth was relatively bare, especially compared to her outfit. It was just a plain tabletop and her tarot deck, no candles or crystals or anything else con artists use to lure in the more gullible patrons. Since her environment wasn't offering any clues, I suggested, "We should find some people who knew her, and talk to them. If she was a witch, odds are some of her friends will be, too."

"I can ask Jill if she's got a list of known associates yet," Dan began, then he leaned closer to the screen. There was another video of our victim in the queue. "Click on that video. The background looks familiar."

I did as asked, and we watched our victim stand in front of a classroom, and give a lecture on the basics of tarot. Never in my life had I come across tarot based curriculum, nor could I imagine what school had hired her. Then the camera panned wide, and I saw the school's logo displayed on the back wall of the classroom.

The video was recorded at Braerton College, where Bennet Carrington, the local shepherd, worked as the school's master horticulturist.

"Holy shit," I said. "She was teaching tarot at Braerton!"

"I guess we know who to talk to next," Dan said. "Let's pay Bennet a visit."

"After we eat," I said. "Don't try to keep me from my pancakes, Lyons."

As it turns out, there's a certain amount of skill involved in flipping pancakes. Dan possessed that skill, and I most certainly did not. He took over after I'd ruined half the batter, and Stuart ended up possessing a belly full of my mangled attempts. Early mishaps aside, our lunch was delicious.

After we finished eating, we headed straight to Braerton College. Luckily, Bennet was in his office when we got there. We found our favorite horticulturist seated behind his desk, poring over a set of blueprints.

"Hey, Bennet," I said, from his office's doorway. "Got a minute?"

"Hello, Eli, Dan," Bennet said. "You know I'm always available to you both. What brings you to the college today?"

"Nothing good, I'm afraid," Dan replied. "We're working a homicide, and one of the victims taught tarot cards here at the college."

"Oh, how awful. However, I don't recall anything relating to tarot being taught here, or any other sort of fortune telling, for that matter." Bennet removed his glasses, polished them, and set them back on his nose. "You're certain the class took place at this school?"

"We have a video," I said, then I pulled out my phone and showed him the recording of Colleen teaching the class.

"Ah," Bennet said, as he watched Colleen gesture and show the cards to her students. "She appears to be part of the school's student activities club. They put on a fair every autumn, which includes things like lectures, short films—"

"Fortune telling." Dan interjected.

"Yes, evidently so. One moment," Bennet said, then he rummaged around in his file cabinet. "Here's the schedule from last autumn's event."

I flipped through the booklet. Our victim went by Shyla Nae in her tarot card alter ego. "Did you go to this fair?" I asked.

"I didn't go to this last one, but I have attended the fair in the past," Bennet replied. "The students put on a rather fine event."

"This club isn't associated with the paranormal research department, is it?" I asked. I'd briefly dated someone associated with that department. Turned out he was using me to learn all about my seer abilities in order to complete his thesis. I ghosted him pretty quick, pun intended.

"As far as I know, they aren't," Bennet replied, to my relief. "The club is made up of mostly undergraduates, whereas the paranormal department consists of masters level coursework."

"Good to know," Dan said, then he jerked his chin toward the blueprints. "Are those plans for the once and future greenhouse?"

"They are, and I don't know how I feel about them," he replied. "Everything is laid out quite efficiently, but something seems off about the design. It has no soul, if that makes any sense."

"It does," I said. "You want an old greenhouse that's seen generations of gardeners and apprentices, with old streaky glass and a wall half held up by vines. The school wants you to stick a brand new concrete slab in the ground, and it feels wrong."

"Why yes," Bennet said. "That's it exactly. I must say, Eli, ever since you've embraced your calling as Mistress of Seers, your insight has been uncanny."

"That's Eli, my uncanny wife," Dan said, his face split by a silly grin. "Now, since I'm not a cop any more, I can't go to the registrar's office and pull a list of enrolled students, in order to determine if any of the victims from our case were students here."

"No, you cannot," Bennet said. "However, if you were to drop such a list on my desk, and I were to find it, I could have a look around."

"Thank you." Dan put a scrap of paper on the desk. Bennet picked it up, and went out to the computer in the side office; like many shepherds, he wasn't a fan of having too much modern technology in close proximity to him. Progressive eyeglass lenses were at the upper end of his comfort level.

While we waited, I peeked at the greenhouse's blueprints. "Think Bennet will set up a poison garden in the new greenhouse?"

"That sounds like a lawsuit waiting to happen." Dan wrapped his arms around me, and kissed my hair. "How are you feeling?"

"I'm good. I could go for an iced coffee."

"Pretty sure you're supposed to limit your caffeine intake while you're pregnant."

"Pretty sure that's not happening." Coffee powered at least fifty percent of my daily functions. Without it, I had the mental capacity of toast. "Besides, all Moores love coffee. Gotta get the baby in on the family traditions right away."

"Baby?" Bennet said, as he reentered the room. "Is someone expecting?"

"Um, yeah." I glanced at Dan, saw him smiling. "We are. You're the first person we've told."

"I am quite honored to hear the news," Bennet said. "Congratulations. You will be excellent parents, I have no doubt about that. I will make the necessary recordings in my ledger when I return home," he added; one of Bennet's duties in the supernatural community was to record births and keep lineages straightened out. Speaking of which...

"While you're recording, you might want to update Dan's entry," I said. "Turns out his grandmother is a seer, and his grandfather is a Greek god."

"That's quite interesting," Bennet said, as he grabbed his notebook. "What are their names, if you don't mind my asking?"

"Esme Tofana, and Boreas," Dan replied.

"Ah, Esme," Bennet said, as he scribbled down the names. "She always was a delight. And... Boreas, did you say?"

"Yep, the west wind himself," Dan replied.

"Of course." Bennet said. "As for your three victims, none of them are enrolled in this school, or in any of our affiliates."

"Thanks for checking," Dan said. "You said my nonna was a delight. You've met her?"

"Only in passing," Bennet replied. "When Esme first came to this country, she spent some time in the area, then she moved on to New York. I'm glad to hear she settled down, and had a family."

"She built herself a pretty good life," Dan said. "We gotta work on our case. See you around, buddy."

We left Bennet to his blueprints and ledgers, and headed toward the stairwell.

"I can't believe you called Bennet buddy," I said. "Crap, we forgot to tell him about the mandrake."

"I'm sure we'll talk to Bennet again soon," Dan said, then he paused when we reached the landing. "Check this out," he said, as he pointed at the bulletin board. "It's a flyer for the student club he mentioned."

"Interesting." I took a picture of it with my phone. "They have a website, too. What are the odds that our other two victims were also associated with this club?"

"It's definitely possible," Dan said. "Or they could have gone to the fair, had their cards read." He glanced at me. "Maybe you can apply to be the next fortune teller."

"I really don't know much about tarot, or seeing the future in general," I replied. "As a seer, I'm always focused on the past."

"That can be our in with these people. We can say we don't know much about tarot, and are willing to learn." Dan tapped the lower left corner of the flyer. "Says here you can take a tarot class at a store right on Main Street. Want to check it out?"

"Let's do it."

THE BLACK HAT

The location on Main Street that offered tarot classes turned out to be a mortal-run magic shop called The Black Hat. The shop was in a large storefront with huge floor-to-ceiling windows in the front; if memory served, the last business in that spot was a soup kitchen. It was cute place, even if there wasn't a shred of actual magic on the shelves or anywhere else in the store.

"It's really that bad?" Dan asked, after I'd given him a litany of what the shop was doing wrong.

"I'm just biased," I whispered back, as we browsed the wall of bulk dried herbs. "I grew up around the real deal. All of this stuff is nothing but parlor tricks."

Dan grunted. "What about these plants? Any of them talking to you?"

"I have never once communicated with a dead plant." I opened the plastic bin of chamomile and sniffed. "Seems like good quality stock, though."

"How can you tell?" Dan asked.

A woman wearing a name tag approached us, and said, "You can determine an herb's quality by smelling it. Even though it's dried, it still smells fresh. Sorry, I didn't mean to eavesdrop."

"No worries," I said. "But your herbs are top quality." I glanced at her name tag; it read Dahlia Evergreen. "We actually came here to ask you about the tarot classes, though."

Dahlia frowned. "I'm not sure when we'll have another class. The person who taught them hasn't been around lately."

I opened my mouth, then Dan shook his head slightly. Right, we couldn't go around acting like police officers and revealing the names of homicide victims while the investigation was ongoing. Instead of asking about the missing tarot teacher, I said, "Has this store been here for a while? I don't think I've ever been in here before."

"We're pretty new to this location, and we're filling a much needed gap in the community," Dahlia said.

"What sort of gap?" Dan asked.

"Magic, of course." She looked around the sales floor, then leaned closer as she continued, "Everyone knows there's a huge witch presence in town. We need to be able to defend ourselves against them."

"Forgive my ignorance, but how can herbs and candles protect against witches?" Dan asked.

"On their own, they can't," Dahlia admitted. "But when you put certain items together, and create the proper rituals, we can harness our own magic."

"Who is we?" I asked. "Is there a magic club, so to speak?"

"I wouldn't call it a club, but we do have meetings." Dahlia went to the front counter, and grabbed a pamphlet. "We meet on every Thursday at noon," she said, as she handed me the paper. "We meet other times, too, but the Thursday meetings are open to newbies."

"Thanks," I said, as I put the pamphlet in my bag. "I'll read it over at home. For now, I think I'm going to grab some candles."

I picked out and paid for three candles, then Dan and I left Magic R Us.

"Why'd you want the candles?" he asked, once we were outside.

"Mostly because I like candles," I replied. "But if someone in that store is trying their hand at spell work, the candles could be evidence. Wax is a pretty stable medium, and good for holding intentions."

"Like when you and Jacob made that oil to prove I wasn't possessed," Dan said.

"Exactly," I replied, then I stopped walking. "I am an idiot. We've been wondering if our victims were witches, when we can just ask Jacob."

"Or Tess," Dan added.

"Tess might know, but Jacob has a database of every known witch," I replied; as the head of the Allwood clan, Jacob packed some magical might. The fact that he'd died almost a year ago wasn't even slowing him down. He accomplished just as much as a spirit as he did when he was a flesh and blood man. "Even if these individuals aren't witches, they might be known associates."

"Want to swing by his place now?"

"Nah. I'll send him an email when we get home." I took Dan's hand, and added, "I'm exhausted. Your kid is wearing me out."

Dan looped me in for a hug and kissed my temple. "Us Lyons kids always had a lot of energy. Why do you think my parents are so thin? They had to run to keep up with us."

"That's terrifying. Hopefully this one will be a couch potato like me."

"If we're lucky, he'll be just like you."

News, and a New Client

When we got back to the house, Eli went straight upstairs for a nap. Since I had no idea how to check the candles she'd bought for residual magic, and I didn't want to work on the case without her, I sent my mother a text.

Dan: Up for a video call?

Patty: Of course.

I hit call, and she picked up on the first ring. "Hey, Ma," I said. "You look great."

"I just had my hair done," she replied. "What's up?"

"Ah, well." I was smiling so hard I could barely talk. "Me and Eli are having a baby."

"Danny! That's wonderful!"

Ma yelled the news to my father, and then to Nonna down in her kitchen, and the four of us had a mini celebration. I'd been on the receiving end of news like this so many times, and while I'd always been happy for whomever was expecting, it was always bittersweet; thanks to my first wife passing at such a young age, I'd given up the dream of having kids a long time ago. Now my dream was coming true, and I'd finally be a father.

When life is good, it's really good.

After I hung up with the Queens crew, I went upstairs in search of Eli. I found her snuggled in bed with Stuart snoring beside her. Her laptop was open on the bed beside her, proof that she was a workaholic. If we started charging by the hour, instead of by the case, no one could ever afford us.

I set the laptop on the nightstand and got in bed beside her. Eli rolled over and slid her arm around me.

"Hey," I said, as I kissed her forehead. "Thought you came up here to sleep."

"I'm at that stage of exhaustion where I'm too tired to sleep." She cracked an eyelid. "That doesn't make sense, does it?"

"It does." I stroked her hair back from her face. "Ma sends her love. And Dad, and Nonna."

"You told them about the baby?"

"I did."

Eli pushed herself up on her elbow and smiled at me. "Good. You were so full of news earlier, you looked like you were going to explode."

I pulled her in for a hug. "What can I say? Next to meeting you, it's the best thing that's ever happened to me."

"Don't you forget it, buddy." Eli kissed my jaw. "I'm going to take a bubble bath. Wanna come?"

"Absolutely." While she went into the bathroom and started the water, I paused to scratch Stuart's ears. "You're gonna be a big brother, you know that?"

"Dan. We are not related to the dog," Eli said from the bathroom.

"Don't listen to her," I said to Stuart, then Eli's laptop chimed. "I think you got an email."

"It's probably from Jacob. Read it for me?"

"Sure." I leaned over, and opened her email. She was right, the notification was a reply from Jacob. He wasn't pleased about our investigation.

Eli,

Thank you for reaching out. While I am not familiar with the three people you mentioned, I have heard those surnames spoken of in passing. I'll have LeClerc do a bit of research as to how our clan has interacted with them in the past. As far as that "magic" shop downtown, I would stay away from it and everyone associated with it. The shop—which originally operated out of Westhampton—was founded a few decades ago by a group of mortals who felt the need to arm themselves against witchcraft. History has taught us that these sorts of groups rarely see anyone's point of view but their own.

I'll be in touch when I know more. In the meantime, please let me know how I can assist.

Jacob

"Babe," I said, as I entered the bathroom. The tub was halfway full, and Eli was about to get in. "Jacob doesn't know the victims, and he says the magic shop is bad news."

"Can't say I disagree. When we were in the shop, Dahlia was ready to grab the pitchforks and rid the town of undesirables." She got in the water, and looked at me expectantly. "Well? Get in."

"Yes, ma'am." I shed my clothes and got into the tub with her. Eli shut off the water, then she moved to my side of the tub and arranged herself against my chest. "Maybe we should drop the case. Jacob said the people behind the shop wanted to arm themselves against witchcraft."

"That's exactly why we should keep investigating," Eli said. "We're bringing a baby witch into the world. We can't have these lunatics running around near our kid."

I leaned back and closed my eyes, as my hand went to Eli's belly. "How do we know he'll be a witch? You always say mortality breeds truer than magic. And don't we have more seer between us, what with your line, and my nonna?"

"That's a good point," she admitted. "However, my mother was a crazy powerful witch before I bound her abilities, and we've also got whatever you inherited from Boreas in the mix. Face it, Dan, whether he's a witch or not, he's going to be special."

I tightened my arms around her. "Yeah, he will be."

We lounged in the tub until the water cooled off, then I tucked Eli in bed and went down to the kitchen. Usually, I had no problems finding something for us to snack on, but the egg debacle from that morning made me wonder what Eli could eat without barfing. I'd just grabbed a box of crackers and a jar of peanut butter when there was a knock at the side door.

That was the one our clients used.

Since I was dressed, I opened it right up. A woman was standing there, her gaze darting around the area as she wrung her hands. "Can I help you?" I asked.

"I'm looking for Eliza Moore," she said. "I need to hire her."

"We have an interest form on our website," I said; I left off how we used that form to weed out any potential criminals and other people who were only out to waste our time. "Since there's only two of us, we can't take every case. After you fill out the form, if we can help you out, we'll be in touch."

"This is Nine Lives Investigations, right?" the woman demanded. "And Eliza takes on weird cases, stuff that involves witchcraft?"

"Where'd you hear that?" I asked, as I crossed my arms over my chest.

"My sister is missing, and I think witchcraft is involved," she replied, as her volume and pitch increased. "Please, you have to help me!"

Normally I had no problem turning people away if we couldn't help them, but when she said her sister was missing I hesitated. I had sisters of my own, and if any of them went missing I'd be a wreck. "Did you file a missing person report?"

"I tried, but the police wouldn't take one," she replied. "They said there wasn't enough evidence to list her as missing."

"That's bunk," I said. "Anyone can file a report at any time."

Eli came up beside me, and set her hand on my arm. "If there's not enough evidence for the police to classify her as missing, why do you think witches are involved?" she asked.

"Not witches," she snapped. "Witchcraft." The woman blinked, and got herself under control. "Colleen fell in with a bunch of people who thought witches were after them, or organizing a revolution, or some nonsense. Now she's missing, and I can't shake the feeling that something bad has happened to her."

I glanced at Eli; our tarot card teacher's real name was Colleen. "Ma'am, please come inside," I said. "My name's Dan Lyons. And you are?"

"Megan Bergquist," she replied, then she turned to Eli. "Are you Eliza? Can you help me?"

"I am Eliza, and we will do everything we can to help you," Eli replied. "Have a seat. Would you like some coffee?"

While Eli got Megan settled at the kitchen table, I called Jill.

"Please tell me you have a lead," Jill said when she picked up.

"Do I ever. Colleen Bergquist's sister is sitting in my kitchen."

"I'll be there in ten."

EXPLOSION!

While Dan made coffee, I had Megan write down everything she could remember about the people her sister had fallen in with. That gave us around ten minutes of focused activity, so I could avoid telling Megan that Colleen was already dead. As delay tactics went, it was pretty lame, but I didn't want to give her any false hope. Despite my reputation for cracking impossible cases, there was no way Megan would ever see her sister again; at least, not alive. As for whether or not I would summon Colleen's spirit for a chat, that remained to be seen.

Finally, Jill arrived. Dan and I went out to the living room while Jill explained to Megan that Colleen had died in what appeared to be a violent manner. Listening to Megan's sobs was awful.

"We had to tell her," Dan said, as he wrapped his arm around my shoulders. "It's tough, but it's the right thing to do."

"I know." I didn't want to keep any information from Megan. I just wish she'd come to us months or weeks ago, and we'd had time to keep Colleen safe from whatever had happened to her. "I wish we could fix this."

"We can't change the past, but we can give Megan closure," Dan said. "Maybe we'll even bring a few people to justice."

"You sound like a cop," Jill said, as she entered the living room. "Megan's ready to talk about the people Colleen knew. I figured you two should sit in."

"Megan's okay with us being there?" I asked.

"She is," Jill replied. "I'll record everything and it can serve as her formal statement, so she won't have to go through this twice."

"That's good of you." I went into the kitchen, and sat at the table across from Megan. Her cheeks and nose were bright pink, but otherwise she'd composed herself. "I'm so sorry."

"Thank you," Megan said. "Officer Sanders said when Colleen was found, she was hanging?"

I nodded. "Behind City Hall."

"That's so... odd," Megan said. "And the killer thought she was a witch?"

"Colleen had a sign pinned to her that said witch," Jill said, as she set down printouts of the driver's license pictures of the other two victims. "Do you recognize either of these people?"

Megan shook her head. "They don't look familiar, but I don't really know who she's been associating with lately." Megan glanced up at me. "Colleen knew I thought they were nuts."

"Because they were using witchcraft?" I prompted.

"Because they thought they were some kind of soldiers in a magic war," Megan replied. "Their leader is a woman—her name escapes me—but she's convinced her followers that they're the last line of defense from whatever these witches have planned for humanity."

"Sounds like a cult," Dan said.

"That's because it is," Megan said. "She would hand out paperwork encouraging people to be righteous, and tell them to strike down evil wherever they find it."

I felt my anger rising; witches had been the scapegoats for mortal woes for thousands of years. This wasn't a new mantra, but I hated it all the same. "Are you familiar with the magic shop on Main Street?" I asked.

"Magic shop?" Megan repeated. "Can you buy spells there?"

"More like items to cast spells," I replied. "We've learned that Colleen was associated with a group that met at the shop. Colleen was also teaching people about tarot cards, and using the name Shyla Nae."

Megan laughed softly. "That was our cat's name, from when we were kids. And she was teaching people about tarot cards? I've never once heard her mention tarot."

"Here." I called up the video on my phone. "This is her at the college."

"Oh, my god." Megan reached toward the screen, then curled her fingers inward. "I barely recognize her. My sister was an accountant. She worked at a finance corporation, helping people with retirement plans and fund transfers. How did she become this person?"

"We'll find out," I said. "Dan, can I talk to you while Officer Sanders finishes up?"

"Sure," Dan said. We returned to the living room, while Jill continued taking Megan's statement. "What's up?"

"Have you ever heard of an anti-witch cult around here?"

"I haven't, and believe me, I'd remember that," he replied. "You never have, either?"

"Never," I said. "Historically, this region has always been open to the supernatural. It's why my family settled here in the first place, then the witch clans followed us from the Old World."

"Then whatever this group is, it's new," Dan said, as he rubbed his chin. "That means it might not have gained too much traction yet."

"It's got enough traction to commit murder," I said, then I heard the kitchen door open and close. A moment later, Jill joined us.

"Having Megan stop by was serendipitous," Jill said. "Not that she has any idea who killed her sister, or any actionable information we can work with."

"If you ask me, this was all a little too convenient," Dan said. "Why did she come here demanding to see Eli? It's not like we advertise that we solve supernatural cases."

"It's definitely suspect," Jill said. "And despite what Megan said, no one attempted to file a missing person report for Colleen, or the other two victims. I checked every department in the county."

"Then she's already lied once," I said. "I wonder what else she lied about?"

"I'll pull Colleen's employment history," Jill said. "Let's see if she really was an accountant. Eli, are they any witchy angles you can exploit?"

"I've already asked the head of the Allwood clan to look into the victims," I replied. "But I still think these people were killed by mortals, not witches."

"If they were mortals who had a grudge against witches, there might be a trail I can follow within the department, and you can pick up in your own way," Jill said.

"My own way?" I repeated. "Jill, all I usually do is talk to ghosts."

"Well, if you see Casper, ask him for some leads," Jill said. "Thanks for calling me in on this, guys. I'll let you know when I have something."

Jill grabbed her files and recorder, and let herself out. I turned to Dan, and said, "I'm going to get our laptops. We need to find out everything there is to know about Megan."

"Agreed," Dan said. "Are you hungry? I can make more pancakes."

"Yes, and now I want peanut butter," I said, as I jogged up the stairs to our bedroom. As I grabbed my and Dan's laptops, I happened to glance out of the window toward the backyard. I'd never noticed I before, but our house was in a direct line with Senator Barbara Stevens's house.

"Did you know that we can see the Stevens house from here?" I asked, when I reentered the kitchen. "It's a straight shot from our bedroom window."

Dan grunted. "I knew that her house was in that direction, but I've never seen it from here. Not that I've ever really looked for it, either. Maybe it's more obvious now, what with the leaves being off the trees."

"Maybe." I set down the computers, and saw the snack platter Dan had put together: a jar of peanut butter, carrot sticks, crackers, and chocolate chip cookies. "When did you do all this?"

"Just now. I need to keep you well fed and happy."

"I'm not a show pony," I said, as I grabbed a cookie. "But this is great. Thank you."

"Any time, baby."

I smiled at my thoughtful husband, and got up to get something to drink. The candles I'd purchased at The Black Hat were sitting on the counter, so I grabbed them and set them next to the food.

"You're not gonna eat those, are you?" Dan asked, as he eyed the candles.

"Why would I eat wax?"

"Pregnant women get weird cravings."

I glared at him. "If I start craving non-food items, you'll be the first to know."

While he chuckled, I lined up the candles. They were all in colorful glass jars, and the tops of the candles were studded with crystals and dried flowers.

"Which one should we light first?" I asked. "We've got love, money, and good health to choose from."

"Let's do health," Dan said. "Any idea how a candle is supposed to make you healthier? Does the flame cure cancer?"

"If only." I unscrewed the jar and smelled the wax. The candle itself was bright yellow and smelled like citrus, which was nice. There were a few yellow and green stones set on the top, along with some dried yellow petals that reminded me of straw flowers. Since it wasn't going to light itself, I snapped my fingers to ignite the wick.

The jar exploded.

I screamed and covered my eyes as Dan flung himself across the table. Carrot sticks and crackers went flying, but instead of hitting us, the wax and broken glass hovered in the air, motionless, like some bad CGI in a science fiction movie.

"Why isn't it moving?" Dan demanded. "What is happening here?"

"I don't know." I lowered my arms, and the candle shrapnel lowered as well. Curious, I reached toward it. The ball of wax and glass stayed approximately six inches away from me at all times, no matter how I moved or stretched.

"Holy shit," I murmured. "Dan, I halted the explosion."

"All right," he said. "Put those shards down before someone gets cut."

"I'm trying." No matter what direction I moved my hand, or how close I got the shards to the table, they remained suspended in the same pattern. On a hunch, I said, "Reform."

Before our eyes, the wax and glass and dried flower petals put itself back together. Even the crystals returned to the same pattern on the candle's surface.

"Oh my god," Dan said. "Did you just undo an explosion, or did you turn back time?"

"I have no fricken' idea." I glanced up at him. "I think we should call Tessa."

"Yeah." Dan pulled out his phone. "Her, and the bomb squad."

PROTECTION

Dan called Tessa while I stashed the explosive candles in the freezer. She arrived about twenty minutes later, and brought my dad along for the ride.

My father and Tessa had an epic on again, off again love affair that began years before I was born. A few decades ago, Tess returned to Italy and stayed there for about five years, and during that time Dad met my mother, the result of which was me. That understandably caused some friction between everyone. But now Dad and Tessa were together again, and everyone was ridiculously happy about it.

Well, everyone was happy except my mother, but she left my dad before I was even born. Her opinion on Dad and Tessa's relationship did not count.

"I'm here," Tessa announced, as she swept into the kitchen like royalty, which she was. Her full name and title was Contessa Isabella della Scala, and back in the day she'd ruled a portion of Italy. Nowadays she was one of the most powerful witches in the New World, and lived a well-earned life of leisure.

Even though she now had a civilian life, Tessa still dressed like a queen. Today, her dark hair was pinned up at the nape of her neck, and she wore a blue silk dress topped with a black cashmere coat. On her feet were black stiletto boots, because winter weather was no reason not to be fashionable.

"Thank the ancestors," I said. "Where's your better half?"

"Here," my dad said, laughing. Thanks to my father's extensive use of magic, he looked about thirty years old, much younger than his actual age of one hundred and seventeen. His father was Indian, which meant he had shiny black hair and brown skin, which was a long way of saying he and I didn't look much alike. I'd gotten his brown eyes, but my wavy hair was pale brown, and my skin was so pale I sizzled like bacon in the summer sun. We also shared a casual sense of style, and gravitated toward jeans and tee shirts no matter the occasion.

"Hey, Dad," I greeted. Stuart got to him before I did, which was typical. "As you can see, we had a kitchen explosion."

"Is that why there are crackers on the floor?" Tessa asked, as she stepped around my dad and the pup. "And carrot sticks?"

"What, you don't like my design choices?" I asked. "Actually, we were having snacks when the candle exploded. Dan threw himself across the table to rescue me, and we've been sweeping up the remains of our food ever since."

"Aww, Dan's your knight in shining armor," Tessa said.

"You know it," Dan called from the mudroom. "Next up, I'm slaying dragons."

"My money's on Dan. Show me the misbehaving candles?" Tess asked. I grabbed them from the freezer and set them on the counter, close to the sink in case we needed to hose them down. "And why were they in the freezer?" she asked.

"In case they randomly exploded again."

"What if they had exploded, and compromised the ice cream?" she pressed.

I gasped, then I narrowed my eyes at Tess. "You're the one who can't live without a bowl of butter pecan before bed."

"Guilty," she said. "You said you purchased these candles from a magic shop on Main Street?"

"Yeah. The person we spoke to went on about some borderline anti-witch propaganda, so I grabbed the candles to see if there were any spells suspended in the wax." I tapped the lid of the yellow candle. "This is the one that exploded."

"And you put it back together?" Tessa picked up the jar and examined it. "The glass is perfect. There isn't a single crack or scratch." She lowered the candle and frowned at me. "When did you get a power boost?"

"I haven't had anything like a boost," I said. "If anything, I'm weaker than normal."

"Weaker?" Dad asked, as he joined us at the counter. "How so?"

"I'm exhausted, food is grossing me out, and everything is annoying," I replied. "Well, you guys aren't annoying. But everything else is."

"Sounds like you're pregnant," Tess said, as she picked up the green candle.

"Um. Yeah. I am."

Tessa set down the candle with a *thunk* as Dad's eyes went wide as saucers. "Bug," Dad said. "Really?"

"Yeah," I said, then he pulled me in for the best hug in the history of hugs. I'd grown up with a small family, but I never minded. My dad was everything to me.

"I'm so happy for you," he said, as he squeezed the life out of me. "Tell me what you need and it's yours. Anything at all."

"I don't think I need anything," I said. "Do I? Honestly, you guys know more about this baby stuff than I do."

"How about an appointment with an obstetrician?" Dan asked from the doorway. He was standing there with the broom and dustpan, hunting for more crumbs lurking in the corners.

"A mortal doctor?" Tessa shook her head. "I really don't see what a mortal could do for her that we couldn't."

"We?" Dan said. "What, are you going to sing Kumbaya and hold hands while Eli gives birth on the kitchen table?"

"Eli is right here," I snapped, my face and neck going hot with rage. I didn't care that Dan was my husband and the father of my baby. I hated it when people spoke about me as if I wasn't standing right fricken' there in front of them.

"Dan," my father said, as he set his hand on my forearm. "This is all new for you and Eli. You two have plenty of time to decide how you want to handle things."

I gave my father some side eye. "Don't you use your mediation skills on me."

"I'm using them on both of you," he said. "Dan, did you witness the candle explode?"

"I did," he replied, as he set the broom aside. "Eli snapped her fingers to light it, and the thing went off like a bomb."

"Then whatever spell is imbued inside the candle was activated when you used magic upon it. It's like a magic detector," Tessa said, as she unscrewed the jar and sniffed the candle. "Oh, this smells atrocious!"

"No, it's nice," I began, then she held it out for me to smell. I nearly gagged.

"I assume the prior scent was more pleasant?" she asked.

"It was all citrusy," I replied. "Now it smells like actual garbage."

Tessa set the candle down. "The scent is brimstone, which was probably the catalyst. This was obviously put together to harm or possibly kill anyone who used magic in its presence. The red candle probably uses cinnabar." She folded her arms across her breast. "Why were you in a magic shop in the first place?"

"Because three people were found hanging behind City Hall, and one of them had a sign pinned to her clothes that read witch," I replied. Tessa's eyes bulged; after everything she'd seen and experienced over the centuries, it was almost impossible to shock her. Witch persecutions always did the trick, no matter how many inquisitions she'd lived through. "And it was written in angry red letters."

"These are the victims," Dan said, as he showed my dad and Tess the victims' pictures on his phone. "We tracked the female individual—she was the one that had the sign on her—first to the college, then to the magic shop. She taught classes on tarot cards."

"Interesting," Tess said.

"Wait, there's more," I said. "Earlier today, the victim's sister showed up at our door demanding we find her sister."

"This is beyond interesting," my dad said. "Did you light the candle before or after this woman came by?"

"After," I said, then I glanced at Dan. "Do you think Megan could have tampered with the candles?"

"I don't see how," Dan replied. "She was never alone. When you went upstairs, I stayed in the kitchen with her, then when Jill came by for her statement, she was with Megan until she left."

"Do you think Jill would have noticed if Megan did something to the candles?" Tess asked.

"Jill notices everything," Dan replied. "She probably knows what brand of toothpaste I use."

"Then the question becomes, are all candles at this shop spelled in a similar manner, or were the spelled ones specifically given to you," Tessa said.

"We could always try lighting the other two, and see what happens," I suggested.

"And because you can stop the explosion, you need to be the one to do it," Dan said, as he shook his head. "You are going to give me a heart attack one of these days, you know that?"

"We will protect her, right Alex?" Tessa said. "You too, Dan."

"Of course," my dad replied. "Eli, whenever you're ready."

"Okay." I shook out my hands. "Here goes." I picked up the red candle, unscrewed the lid and held it at arm's length, and snapped my fingers. As expected, it exploded.

Tessa screeched something in Italian as my father yanked me backward. The shattered glass and red wax remained suspended in a ball about a foot in diameter, but just like the last explosion, the shrapnel moved when I moved.

"Here's the really weird part," I said, as my father and Tess stared, mesmerized, at the floating shards of glass and wax. "Watch how the debris follows me." I demonstrated how the shrapnel mimicked my movements, and always remained a constant distance from me.

"You're not controlling this," my dad said. "It's the baby."

I lowered my arm, sending the shrapnel cloud almost to the floor. "How can the baby be doing anything?"

"It's not just the baby," Tessa said. "What's happening is that because you're pregnant, you've got a heightened protection field around you. It should remain in place for the duration of your pregnancy, and for a few months after birth."

"Really." I held my hands in front of me, amazed that such a thing was possible, and accidentally sent the shrapnel cloud hurtling toward Dan. "Sorry!"

"It's okay, babe," Dan said. "Are you saying that for the next year or so, Eli's bulletproof?"

"The protection isn't quite strong enough to stop a bullet," Tessa replied. "But it will repel minor annoyances, like mosquitos or poison ivy, and any sort of magical attack."

"This is so cool," I said. "Oh, and check this out. Reform!"

As quickly as it had shattered, the candle put itself back together. Tessa picked it up and examined it like she had the yellow one.

"Eliza Jayne, you have had a power boost," Tessa declared. "I think it's hereditary. Wasn't Christina also more powerful than usual while she carried you?"

"She was," my dad affirmed. "Christina could change the weather with a thought, and flowers sprang up wherever she walked."

"And we know how plants like to talk to Eli," Dan said. "Speaking of which, there were at least a dozen mandrake plants found at the homicide scene. Eli brought one home."

"Were they beneath the hanged bodies?" Tess asked.

"Some of them were, which reinforces my theory that the victims weren't actual witches," I said. "It's pretty easy to find the lore about mandrake growing beneath a hanged man, but whoever did this scattered mandrakes all across the murder scene. They didn't stop to think that it's the middle of February, and all the plants we found are mature and were plopped into freshly dug holes. Whoever planted them forgot that there is no way they could have grown that much in the few hours since the victims died, especially in winter."

"Can you buy mandrakes at a regular garden shop?" Dan asked.

"Maybe, but would a garden shop have any this time of year?" I shook my head. "The killer planned to make a spectacle of these people, and they planned it for a long time."

"Makes sense," Dan said. "What's our move?"

Tessa tapped the red candle's lid. "Did you get a receipt for these?"

"Yeah. It's in my wallet."

"Return these two because they stink," she said, then she grabbed the green candle. "If you don't mind, I'd like to work on this one and try to reverse engineer whatever was done to it."

"Can you return a candle?" I wondered.

"It doesn't matter, but the staff's reaction to seeing these candles again will speak volumes," Tessa said. "That way, you'll know if the whole store was in on this little magic detecting trick, and if these candles were in any way intended for you."

"Tomorrow's Thursday," Dan added. "They have a get together for people every Thursday at noon."

"A get together? At a mortal run magic shop?" Tessa shook her head. "It sounds like a way to trap witches. If you do go there, stay vigilant, and act mortal."

"I am mortal," Dan said.

"Actually, you should let Dan do most of the talking," my dad said to me, then he turned to Dan. "You're still fascinated by magic to a certain degree. Lean into that, and ask lots of questions. Make them explain to you exactly what they're doing, and why."

"Play up the scared father angle," Tessa added. "After all, you've got a baby to protect."

Dan held out his arm, and I fit myself against him. "Don't you worry," Dan said. "I can play dumb with the best of them. If all else fails, I'll tell stories from when I was a beat cop in Queens."

"That's my husband, the most regular guy in town," I said, as I grinned up at Dan.

"Just be careful," my father said. "And remember that your protection field is limited. I don't want anything happening to my first grandchild."

"Don't worry," I said, as I set my hand on my belly. "We'll take good care of him."

THE GATHERING

Thursday at noon, we arrived at The Black Hat. When Dahlia spotted us, she smiled.

"Do serial killers smile?" I whispered to Dan.

"Behave," he whispered back.

"Hey, guys," Dahlia said, as we approached the front counter. "Are you here for the gathering?"

"That, and I wanted to ask you about these candles I got yesterday," I said, as I pulled the two that had exploded and reformed out of my bag and set them on the counter. "Are they supposed to smell like this?"

"The scents should be citrus and rose," Dahlia said, then she opened the rose candle and grimaced. "That is rank!"

"Okay, so I'm not crazy," I said. "The green candle smelled great, but these two are something else."

"I can refund you," Dahlia began.

"Nah, it's my fault for not smelling them in the store," I said. "I just wasn't sure if they were supposed to be like this."

"Believe me, this smell is not normal," Dahlia said. "Grab two more, and I'll talk to the owner about what happened with these two."

"Oh, I thought you were the owner," I said. "You're so knowledgeable about your products."

"Thanks, but no, I just handle the front of the store," Dahlia said. "Our owner will be at the gathering, though. You guys can meet her there."

I glanced up at Dan. "What do you say? Still want to check it out?"

"Whatever you want, babe," he replied, then he held out his hand to Dahlia. "We never introduced ourselves when we were in here yesterday. I'm Dan, and this is my wife, Eli."

"It's nice to formally meet both of you," Dahlia said. "Have you lived in town for a while?"

"Eli has, but I'm a New Yorker," Dan said.

"Not anymore," I pointed out.

"You can take the boy out of Queens, but you can't Queens out of the boy," Dan said, as I rolled my eyes. "Ever get down to the city, Dahlia?"

"Oh, no. This is probably the closest I've ever been to New York." She retrieved a set of keys from underneath the register, then she locked the front door. "The gathering's in the basement. Follow me."

Dan glanced at me. I shrugged, and we followed Dahlia down the stairs to what hopefully wasn't a murder room. He leaned close to my ear, and murmured, "I brought my gun."

"Dan! Why did you do that?"

"Just in case." When I kept glaring at him, he added, "This reeks of the time I followed you to Beauclaire's house and we ended up tied up in the basement."

I remembered waking up on the cold hardwood floor, with my hands tied to Dan's behind my back. "Was that the first time you rescued me?"

"Yeah, and my good deed got me smacked in the face with a coffee mug." He kissed my hair. "But it was all worth it, for you."

We entered the basement, which was a bright white space reminiscent of a classroom. There was a whiteboard on the far wall, folding chairs set up in a circle on one side of the room, and a table with refreshments on the other. About a dozen other people were milling around, making small talk and presumably plotting the end of witchcraft as we know it.

Dahlia started introducing us, and I was happy to let Dan handle most of the talking. He leaned into his nice guy detective persona, and asked genial yet probing questions of everyone who would talk to us. He avoided the subjects of magic and witchcraft entirely, which was smart. You never ask someone outright if they're a bigot. You wait for them to volunteer the information themselves.

"Aren't you the PIs who handle the weird cases?" one man asked us. His name tag said Ron.

"That is a rumor, and it's all my fault," I said. "I rescued a girl that had been abducted, and no one could figure out how I managed to do something the cops and the FBI couldn't. A reported asked me if I used magic to find her, and I said yes." I gave Ron a sheepish smile. "I was being sarcastic, but the reporter ran with it."

"So how'd you find the kid?" Ron asked.

"Dumb luck," I replied. "I pulled into a gas station, and the people who'd kidnapped her were already there. They let her go into the restroom. I followed her in, and asked her if she wanted me to take her home."

"That's some luck," Ron said. "I bet that kid was pretty thrilled you were there."

"So yeah, some of our cases are weird," Dan said, thankfully steering the conversation away from me. "But we crack them all with good old-fashioned detective work."

Ron and the rest murmured their approval. Seeing his moment to shine, Dan launched into a story about a case he worked in Queens from when he was fresh out of the academy. While he entertained the crowd, I investigated the refreshment table.

"Your husband sure is a talker," Dahlia said, as I claimed a water bottle from the cooler.

"You should see him right after he has some coffee," I said. "But yeah, Dan loves people. He'll know everyone's life story by the time we leave."

"That's great," Dahlia said. "Have you tried any of the snacks? We have brownies!"

"Really." Brownies were my absolute favorite treat in the world. I leaned in for a closer look as I twisted the cap on my water bottle, but I didn't hear the distinctive snap of the plastic breaking. I glanced down, and verified that the seal had already been broken, but not by me.

Someone had spelled the candles, and it looked like the water had been tampered with, too. That meant the snacks were probably unsafe, as well. Dammit, I really wanted a brownie.

"Here you go," Dahlia said, as she handed me a square of fudgy decadence on a paper napkin. "Oh, looks like we're about to start."

"Great, I'll just grab Dan," I said, as I accepted the brownie. Maybe Tessa could test it for residual magic.

Dan was clear on the other side of the basement, entertaining people with stories of his life in Queens. I set my hand on Dan's elbow, and he tore himself away from his fan club so we could find some seats.

"You're popular," I said.

"Surprised?" he said, and I laughed. Then he reached for the water bottle balanced in the crook of my elbow.

"No," I said, as I looked him dead in the eye. "At home."

"Okay," he said; man, I hoped he wasn't too thirsty. "Is the brownie off limits, too?"

"Definitely." I wrapped up the brownie in the napkin and stashed it in my bag, then the person Dahlia referred to as the store owner entered the room. I got a look at her face, and almost fainted.

"Is that…" Dan began.

"Yeah. It's her." Leading the anti-witch gathering was none other than Cecily Allwood.

The person standing at the front of the room, telling us in grandiose detail why we needed to remain vigilant against the magic users in our community, looked and sounded exactly like Cecily Allwood, but it wasn't her. How was I certain of this? She'd looked directly at Dan and me multiple times, and hadn't recognized us. Being that we were responsible for uncovering her plot to take over the Allwood clan, her involvement in the murder of her brother, Jacob, and her subsequent imprisonment and loss of her powers, I was pretty sure she remembered what we looked like.

Which meant the person at the front of the room was a fake Cecily. But why would anyone bother with that?

"We must keep up the pressure against those who would use magic against us," the fake Cecily said. "Have you ever wondered why you didn't get a job when you were a perfect fit for the role, or why your lawn turned brown or a pet ran away? It could have been coincidence. Bad things happen to us all, right? But it also could have been someone using witchcraft to further themselves at the expense of us. Us! Hard working, law abiding, *mortals*." She shook her head. "They have an unfair advantage, and we need to stop them."

Dan took my hand. I'd clenched mine into a fist so tight my knuckles were white. I relaxed my fingers and laced them with his. "This is so weird," I whispered.

"Hang tight, babe," he whispered back. The fake Cecily wrapped up her speech as Dahlia set out a stack of flyers.

"Everyone, grab one of these on your way out," Dahlia said, as she waved one of the flyers over her head. "It's got the date and location of our next investigation."

"Investigation into what?" I whispered.

"Let's go be friendly," Dan murmured, then he strode up to Dahlia. "What's this about an investigation?"

"We have reason to believe an individual in town is using witchcraft," Dahlia said. "He's known to be at this location on Saturday mornings, so we're all going to converge on the area and see if anything out of the ordinary happens."

"Hey, like a good old fashioned stakeout," Dan said with a grin. This guy was on track to win an Oscar. "What do you say, babe? Want to tag along?"

"I don't know," I said, shaking my head. Out of the corner of my eye, I saw fake Cecily quietly leave the room. "It sounds awful dangerous. I don't want to get in any trouble."

"You won't," Dahlia said. "This is a public place, so we're well within our rights to go there. And we're not going to confront the guy, no matter what happens. We're just going to observe."

I glanced at the address printed on the flyer. It was for a bookstore that had an attached bakery and café. "I guess it wouldn't hurt if we went out for breakfast."

"That's the spirit, babe," Dan said, then he handed Dahlia one of our cards. "We'll be there. If anyone needs a ride, let us know."

"Thanks," Dahlia said, as she pocketed the card. "See you Saturday!"

We waved our goodbyes, and headed outside through a door in the rear of the basement. It let us out into the alley behind the shops, close to the parking area. That was convenient.

"Why couldn't I have any water?" Dan asked when we were in the car.

"The seal was broken when I picked it up," I replied. "It might be spelled. Why did you give Dahlia our card?"

"Look there." He pointed toward a spot next to the door marked Employee Parking. "See how that spot's empty? Seems like Dahlia doesn't have a car. If she hits us up for a ride on Saturday, not only do we get to see where she lives. We'll also get some time alone with her in the car."

I was impressed. "You're a pretty good detective, you know that? Ever think about doing this professionally?"

Dan laughed. "Carmelo keeps trying to get me back on the force. He wants to recruit you, too."

"Oh, that's a bad idea," I said. "I don't do well with authority. You were a great police officer, though."

He kissed the back of my hand. "Thanks, baby. Want to head over to Jacob's?"

I thought about the fake Cecily we'd just listened to for an hour. "That is a great idea."

The Allwood Compound

We pulled up to the vast Allwood Compound about thirty minutes after we left The Black Hat. Jacob's house also doubled as the headquarters for his clan, and it sat on a hill overlooking most of the city. Even if you were new in town, with one look at this mansion, you'd know that some major players were hanging out in this place.

I used to hate coming up here. Back when Eli first started opening up to me about the magical parts of her life, and I helped her solve the case of who murdered Jacob Allwood, I got bagged by some of Cecily's goons and beaten within an inch of my life. They left me in the compound's basement as bait for Eli. My girl found me, and rescued me, and together we sent Cecily away to a mortal prison for a long, long time. So while I used to have borderline panic attacks whenever we pulled up to the Allwood place, now I made a point of concentrating on all the good things that happened here.

Me and Eli's first kiss also happened right here, next to the basement door. So yeah, most of my memories of this place were pretty good.

After we got past security, Jacob himself met us in the foyer. He'd been dead for almost a year, but Eli had used her seer abilities to give him some sort of a spiritual power boost that made him as solid as a living man. She referred to Jacob as a "robust spirit". I thought the whole thing was a little creepy, but at least Jacob was a good guy who used his extra time here on earth to look after his family.

I glanced at Eli. She'd always been powerful, and now that she was pregnant, she had some kind of bubble of protection surrounding her. I hoped she wouldn't get cocky, and run off and do something dangerous. At least, not without taking me along for the ride.

"Wonderful to see you two," Jacob greeted. "Let's go up to the office. How have you been doing?"

"Great," Eli replied. "There's a woman who looks exactly like your sister running an anti-witch movement in town."

Jacob stopped dead in his tracks, no pun intended. Maybe a little intended. "Cecily is doing this?"

"We don't think it's her," I replied. "Mainly because she didn't recognize us. But this woman is a dead ringer for your sister."

Jacob nodded, and led us into his office. His assistant, Jacques LeClerc—who was also dead, but hey, we didn't discriminate—was sitting behind the desk. "LeClerc, please contact the prison and ask after Cecily. I need assurance that she's alive and in her cell."

"Alive?" LeClerc repeated. "We haven't been notified otherwise."

"Please," Jacob said. "Humor me."

"Of course," LeClerc said, then he left the room, presumably to make some calls. Jacob took the seat LeClerc had vacated and tapped a pencil on the desk's surface.

"You didn't happen to get a picture of this individual, did you?" he asked.

"Unfortunately, no," I replied. "But I'm pretty convinced it's not her."

"This individual also owns a mortal run magic shop," Eli added. "I bought a few candles from them, and they exploded when I used magic to light the wick. Also, they gave us refreshments at their anti-witch meeting, and the water bottles weren't sealed. I brought one over to see if you could detect anything weird."

Eli set the water bottle on Jacob's desk. He frowned, and waved his hand over the top. The water glowed a sickly yellow.

"Interesting," he murmured. "The water changes color in the presence of magic."

"Like a litmus test gone wrong," I muttered. "Would it have hurt Eli if she drank it?"

"Unsure," Jacob replied. "Based on the fact that the candles exploded, I think it would be best to avoid all food and drink supplied by these people."

"I got a brownie from the refreshment table, too," Eli said, then she put the squashed treat on the desk. "Sorry. It got a little mangled in my bag."

Jacob waved his hand over the brownie. Nothing. "It appears to be a mundane dessert, but I would still advise against eating it," Jacob said. "If they'll tamper with water, nothing they provide is safe."

"I agree," I said as I swept the crumbs off the desk and into my hand, and tossed the whole thing into the trash. "As you've probably guessed, we're wondering if the people associated with this store have anything to do with the bodies that were found behind City Hall."

"These meetings would be one way to source victims," Jacob said. "Or accomplices."

LeClerc reentered the office. "Cecily is alive, but currently in solitary confinement," he said. "Apparently, she entered into a romantic relationship with one of her guards, who has since been fired."

"Go Cecily," Eli said. When the rest of us looked at her, she asked, "What? Good for her for finding love in adverse circumstances."

"Oh, Eli," Jacob said, as he shook his head. "Do you have the name of this guard?"

"Arthur Wexford," LeClerc replied. "I have a copy of his file being delivered by courier now."

"That was one of our victims," I said. "So this guy meets Cecily, gets himself fired when they get too close, and ends up in a staged witch execution?"

"This is getting crazy, even for us," Eli said, as she pulled out her phone. "The magic store doesn't have a website. I'm pulling up the property records."

"Do you have a cause of death for the victims yet?" Jacob asked.

"We don't, and despite how they were found, I don't think they died by hanging," I replied. "Is mandrake poisonous?"

"Yes, it's quite deadly," Jacob replied. "Why do you ask?"

"Someone planted about a dozen mandrakes all around where the bodies were left," I replied. "Eli snagged one."

Both Jacob and LeClerc had expressions of utter disbelief on their faces. Before either one of them could speak, Eli made an announcement.

"Our magic shop, The Black Hat, is owned by Francesca Wexford," she said. "Gonna go out on a limb and suggest that she's related to our guy Arthur."

Jacob nodded, then he turned to LeClerc. "Get me all of those property records, and anything else you can find with the name Wexford," he said. LeClerc dipped his chin, and slipped out of the room. Once he was gone, Jacob wiped his hand down his face.

"Dismiss this as the hope of an old man, if you'd like, but I don't feel like Cecily is involved in this," he said. "Compared to her past schemes, this is crude and ham fisted. To leave three corpses out in the open is not something she would do."

"Her powers are bound," I pointed out. "That could be making her desperate, and resorting to schemes she wouldn't ordinarily try."

"I agree with Jacob here," Eli said. "Everything about this points to a badly informed mortal trying way too hard to make the victims look like witches. The only thing the victims were missing were pointy hats and broomsticks."

"Exactly. We witches like to think we have finesse," Jacob said. "When you were at this magic shop, did you speak to the person masquerading as Cecily?"

"We didn't," I replied. "Come to think of it, she talked at us for a while, but I didn't see her have a conversation with anyone."

"The individual could have been wearing a glamour," Jacob said. "The magic is quite fragile, and can shatter if pressed too hard. She may have memorized her speech, and avoided unplanned conversations so as not to tax the spell."

"Then we're back to a poorly trained mortal using magic against witches," Eli said. "This all seems like a lot of effort just to kill three people. Whoever's behind this must have a massive agenda."

"Agreed," Jacob said. "And agendas like this require funding. In the Old Country, witch hunts were financed by royalty."

"So glad we don't have a monarchy here," Eli muttered. "But you've got a point. We need to follow the money. So, who's the equivalent of a king around here?"

"We may not have kings, but we do have politicians," I said. "Didn't Jill tell us that the senator's sister is running for mayor?"

"Yeah, and Barbara endorsed the other side." Eli glanced at Jacob. "While I wouldn't put Barbara Stevens on the same level as the British Empire, she is loaded."

"I'm aware," Jacob said. "We're passing acquaintances, though I can't say I've ever met her sister."

"What do you say, Eli?" I asked. "Want to make an appointment to catch up with your buddy Barbara?"

"Can't hurt," she replied. "Let's do it."

INNER SPACE

Eli: Hi! Dan and I are working a case, and we were wondering if we could talk to you about it.

Barbara: Does it involve me?

Eli: Not at all, but the victims were found behind City Hall. We want to make sure we're not overlooking anything, political-wise.

Barbara: Understood. I'll check my calendar and get back to you.

I set down my phone and glanced at Dan. "Barbara's going to talk to her people, then her people will call our people, and we'll get together."

"Sounds good," he said, as he turned into the parking lot. We were downtown again, officially to grab ourselves a late lunch. Unofficially, we wanted to snoop around City Hall and the attached park slash murder scene. "Did you mention her sister?"

"Nope. I told her we were working a case, and said we needed to look at it from a political angle. I didn't want to spook her over what might be nothing."

"Good job." He flashed me a smile, then he pulled into a parking spot. "What do you want for lunch?"

"I don't know. Let's take a walk and see what doesn't turn my stomach." We exited the car, and Dan wrapped his arm around my shoulders. "Anything happening at the park?"

Dan looked toward City Hall, and the park that abutted it. "Looks like business as usual."

I shuddered. "I feel bad for everyone that works there. Having corpses turn up at your job is the worst."

"Especially for the corpses." We crossed the street, and paused in front of the entrance to the park. Some of the mandrakes that we assumed had been planted by our killer were in view, all wilted and near death from being out in the frigid February wind.

"When we get home, remind me to check on our mandrake," I said, hoping it had recovered from being transplanted twice in as many days, and wanted to talk. "Maybe it—"

Tires squealed, then an impact sounded. Pain exploded across my back, and the world went dark.

When I came back to myself, I was cold. And a bit woozy.

Had I been drinking?

No, of course not. I rarely drank alcohol, mostly because it screwed with my foresight. And I wouldn't drink while I was—

My memories came at me in a rush: standing on the sidewalk with Dan, the car accident, the noise and pain.

My baby.

I put my hand on my belly. It didn't feel any different, so I guessed that was good. I tried to roll onto my side, and discovered about a billion tubes and wires stuck into me. The top half of my body was wearing a hospital gown, though I still had my jeans and socks on.

So. I was a patient in a mortal hospital. That couldn't be good. I felt around for the nurse call button, and came up empty.

"Hey." Dan appeared next to me, and caressed my cheek. "Don't try to move too much. What do you need?"

"What happened?" I worked my cold fingers between his warm ones. "Why... why hospital?"

"You know those stone pillars at the entrance to the park?" he asked, and I nodded. The pillars had always reminded me of a set at the Pere Lachaise cemetery in Paris. "A guy lost control of his car and hit one of the pillars. The thing shattered, and a massive hunk of stone hit us."

"Oh." I willed my eyes to focus on Dan's face. He didn't look like he'd been hit with a few tons of stone. "Are you okay?"

"I'm okay. You took the brunt of it." He stroked my hair with one hand, while the other held mine as if he thought I'd disappear at any moment. "You shoved me out of the way. The paramedics were shocked you survived."

I swallowed hard; I remembered hearing the accident, but nothing else. "Shocked?"

"Yeah. When the dust settled, you were unconscious under all the debris from the pillar. The rocks were so heavy..."

"You dug me out?" I asked, certain I'd misunderstood.

"Yeah. I did." Dan kissed my forehead. "Don't ever try that again. Save yourself, not me."

"Not agreeing to that." Now that I'd been awake for a bit, whatever drugs the hospital had pumped in me were wearing off. "I'll keep saving you whenever you need it. Besides, I'm okay. We're okay."

"You sure?"

I turned my awareness inward, and felt the spark that was our baby. "I'm sure. He's warm and happy."

"Him?" Dan asked, grinning. "You sure?"

I grinned back. "Pretty sure."

The curtain around my bed snapped back. A man wearing blue scrubs and a white coat was standing there, clipboard in hand. I guessed he was the doctor. "Mrs. Lyons?"

"That's me." I pushed myself to sit up. Dan fluffed the pillows behind my back like a professional butler. "What can I do for you?"

"It's more what I can do for you," he replied. "I'm Dr. Besami. How are you feeling?"

"A little chilly." I held up the arm with the IV in it. "Exactly what are you putting into me?"

"That's just saline," Dr. Besami replied. "Earlier, we gave you something for pain, and we took some blood."

I glanced at Dan. I was certain he wouldn't have let the doctors do anything to me I wouldn't have approved of, but I did not like having a vial of my blood hanging around the hospital. "So, what's your diagnosis? Will I live?"

"Definitely," he replied. "After what happened, both you and your husband are remarkably uninjured. You were knocked unconscious, but you don't have any signs of a concussion. No contusions or lacerations, either."

"Great! Does that mean I'm free to go?"

"Well, yes, but the bloodwork revealed that you're about thirteen weeks pregnant," Dr. Besami said. "I'd like to do an ultrasound, just to verify that all's well with the baby."

Thirteen weeks. I hadn't thought I was that far along, but all I had to go by was some magic smoke that showed me a baby's face. Even though I disliked mortal medical practices, an ultrasound was a good idea. "Um, okay," I said, as I tightened my grip on Dan's hand. "Where will this ultrasound take place?"

"We can do it right here. Hang on." Dr. Besami stepped away, I assumed to make a few preparations for this ultrasound. I looked down at myself, then at Dan.

"This whole baby thing just got very real," I said. "I had no idea about this thirteen weeks business."

Dan sighed. "At this rate, we might not make it for the rest of the weeks."

"We'll be fine," I said. "Protection bubble, remember?"

He stroked my hair back from my forehead. "Let's not test how strong that bubble is, okay?"

The doctor returned, pushing a cart that held a white machine with a few attachments and a small screen; I must have looked confused, because Dan whispered in my ear that it was the ultrasound machine. Dr. Besami picked up a tube, and said, "If you'll just lift up your gown, we'll put some of this jelly on your stomach and get started."

I pulled up the gown and unbuttoned my jeans, then Dr. Besami spread the icy cold gel on me. As soon as I was properly lubed up, he pressed a wand to my belly. On the screen, a swirl of gray and black appeared.

"That looks like outer space," I said.

"Inner space, actually," he said, as he moved the wand around. "Ah. See that?" He pointed to a rapidly moving blob. "That's the heartbeat."

"Oh." I covered my mouth with my hand, my heart suddenly overfull. Nothing could have prepared me for seeing that tiny, tangible proof of my baby. "Dan, he has a heartbeat."

"Yeah, he does." Dan kissed the side of my head. "He's perfect."

"This your first?" Dr. Besami asked.

"He is." I glanced at the doctor, and back at the screen. "He's okay, right? No contusions or lacerations?"

Dr. Besami laughed. "None at all. This is one very healthy fetus you're carrying, Mrs. Lyons. Who's your obstetrician?"

"I don't have one." When Dr. Besami frowned, I added, "That's bad, isn't it?"

"Yes and no," he replied. "You've been very lucky so far, but having regular checkups will ensure that both of you stay as healthy as possible. I'll write a referral for you and include it with your discharge paperwork."

"Thank you, doctor," I said, as I stared at the screen. Despite my earlier attitude about mortal doctors, one had just shown me my baby, and proven he was safe and unharmed. Maybe the obstetrician wouldn't be so bad, after all.

Dinner, Finally

It took about thirty minutes for my discharge paperwork to be completed. In that time, Dan located my shoes, though the remains of my coat and shirt were nowhere to be found. According to Dan, the paramedics had cut them off me. That was irritating, though I did appreciate the effort, and at least my jeans had been spared. Anyway, Dan offered me his sweatshirt, since he had a tee shirt on underneath. His coat had also remained intact.

"It wasn't me they were concerned about," he explained, when I asked him why he hadn't gotten the full EMT experience. "As soon as I told them you're pregnant, they went into full lifesaving mode."

"You're always looking out for me," I said, as I stretched up to kiss his stubbly jaw. We were standing in the lobby waiting for our ride, who just happened to be Jill. Dan had called her to let her know about the accident, and she offered to pick us up and bring us back to our car. "I'm surprised she has time to chauffeur us around."

"Jill's a good one. She makes time when she's needed." Dan wrapped his arm around my shoulders. "You sure you're warm enough?"

"I'm okay," I replied, and that was just weird. I hated the cold, and normally shivered any time the temperature dropped below seventy degrees. The fact that I was wearing one layer in February and not complaining about imminent frostbite was quite unusual. Instead of worrying about that, for now, I peered out of the lobby windows at the parking lot. "Hey, there she is."

We flagged down Jill, and hopped into her car. Dan even let me have the front seat.

"Are you guys okay?" Jill asked. "I went by the accident scene on the way here. It's pretty gnarly."

"We're good. I have discharge paperwork," I added, as I held up my forms.

Jill shook her head. "Eli, I wish I had your energy and enthusiasm. Anyway, as I'm sure you've both deduced, the timing of this accident is beyond coincidental."

"Really?" I hadn't deduced a thing, but I had been knocked unconscious and given mortal drugs. Who knew how much they'd dulled my senses. "How so?"

"Since the city was founded in sixteen fifty-four, not a single corpse has turned up at a municipal property," she began. "The other day, we had three. Also, those pillars at the park entrance have been standing for over one hundred years. Today, they were demolished."

"And we're the common denominator," Dan finished. At least his brain was still working. "We got called in to consult on the case, and then we were standing in front of the pillars. Someone doesn't want us figuring out how or why the victims ended up there."

"No, they do not," Jill agreed. "Have you guys turned anything up?"

"We went back to the magic shop, and attended one of their anti-witch gatherings," I replied. "Hey, can you get property records for that parcel?"

"Yeah. Just text me the address. Do you need anything else from me, case-wise?"

"The people from the shop are running an actual witch hunt on Saturday," I said, as I pulled out my phone. Luckily, Dan had held onto my bag after the accident. "It's at the bookstore on Masonic Avenue. They're staking out a man who supposedly uses witchcraft."

Jill frowned. "That's not good. It sounds like they're one step away from erecting a gallows in the town square. Did you get the man's name?"

"They never mentioned his name," Dan said. "Eli and me are going to show up, and keep an eye on everything."

"Want to come along?" I asked. "It can be a brunch date. Angel would love it."

"She would," Jill agreed. "However, she's working Friday night, so she won't be up for a Saturday morning stakeout. I'll be available, though. Here we are."

Jill pulled up next to our car. "Call me if you need backup," she said as we got out of her vehicle, then she drove off. I leaned on Dan, and felt waves of hunger emanating from my stomach.

"We never got lunch," I said.

"What do you want, baby?" he asked. "Pancakes, cereal, toast?"

"I want Greek food," I said. "Something with spinach and feta and a ton of tzatziki sauce. And pita bread!"

"Want to go home, and order it from that place you like?"

"Sure."

We got in the car, and Dan headed toward our house.

"You know," I began, "the house is like your version of a protection bubble."

"Yeah? How's that?"

"You don't want me out in the world where I could get hurt, so you're bringing me to the one environment where you can control everything," I replied. "Well, everything except Stuart."

"He is an unpredictable pup," Dan said, as he navigated through an intersection. I noticed that he was taking the long way home, and deliberately not driving by City Hall. "And yes, I do want you safe at home. You may have a protection bubble, but you have more than just you to worry about right now."

I had nothing to say to that, since he was right. And even if this protection bubble or whatever it was kept me alive, my baby could still be hurt. Besides, I liked it when Dan took care of me.

"You're right," I said. "I guess we'll be seeing that mortal doctor soon, huh?"

"You bet your ass."

"My ass has nothing to do with this."

"That's where you're wrong, babe." His gaze slid toward me, then back to the road. "That ass started all of this."

I laughed as I pulled up the Greek restaurant's website. "Keep driving, you goof. What do you want for dinner?"

When we got back to the house, Dan handled Stuart while I took a shower. Since I'd just gotten out of the germy hospital, I decided to treat myself to the shower in the downstairs bathroom. It may not seem like using the bathroom on the first floor as opposed to the second would make much of a difference, but the downstairs shower was bigger, and the showerhead was lower. When you're short like me, stuff like that matters.

After my long, hot, super steamy shower, I emerged into the attached guest bedroom and found Dan waiting for me. Our food had been delivered, and he'd spread it out on the bed like a picnic.

"This is nice," I said, as I tucked my towel under my arms and sat on the edge of the bed. "Where's the hummus?"

"Right here," Dan said, as he handed me the plastic container, and a foil packet with warm pita bread. "Hey, you're dripping."

I glanced at the still-wet hair plastered to my shoulder. "Sorry. I didn't know we were having dinner in here." Dan grabbed a second towel from the bathroom, and blotted my hair. I leaned back, and said, "You know, I could get used to this treatment."

"Then get used to it." He kissed my forehead, then he went back to his side of the bed. "I've got spanakopita over here."

"Give." I opened the container and jammed my fork into the flaky, cheesy goodness. Heaven. "This is the best dinner ever, though I may only feel that way because I'm starved. What time is it?"

"Almost ten. We were in the hospital for a while." I saw his jaw tighten, his only tell.

"Hey." I reached across the bed and put my hand on his arm. "We're all okay. You can relax."

"No, I can't." Dan shook his head. "I didn't see that car coming. I should have been more alert, more aware of my surroundings."

"You can't blame yourself for the car accident," I said. "We have no idea what happened with that guy. He could have had bad brakes, had a heart attack—"

"He was dead," Dan said flatly. "The paramedics were spooked, because it looked like he'd been dead for a while. As in, several weeks, or longer." His words chilled me, ruining the warm glow I'd gotten from the shower.

"Why didn't you tell me this earlier?" I demanded.

"Why? Let's see. My pregnant wife was hit by a ton of stone shrapnel and buried under a heap of rubble, unconscious, and I had no idea if you were even alive under there," he said, his voice rising at the end. "At the time, the dead driver didn't seem important."

He looked up, saw me staring at him. "I'm sorry," he said. "I shouldn't be yelling like that. I was just..."

His voice trailed off. I crawled across the bed, carefully avoiding the food, and wrapped my arms around him. Technically, I was more powerful than Dan. I could create fire with a thought, talk to the dead, and do a whole host of other amazing things. But he was my protector. Always would be.

"You can yell if you want," I said, with my face pressed against his neck. "It's scary when people you love get hurt. I remember when the demon possessed you, and I had to dump a bowl of salt down your throat to get it out." I squeezed my eyes shut, remembering Dan's cold, limp body after the demon had vacated his form. I'd been desperate to save him, so desperate I did something I'd never even considered before that moment.

"I was so worried you wouldn't survive," I whispered. "But I wasn't about to let you go. I reached out into the void and grabbed your spirit, and shoved you back into your body. No way was I going to let you move on before we got our time together."

"I remember," he said. "It was cold and dark, and I'd been screaming your name for what felt like a hundred years. Then I felt you." Dan nuzzled my neck. "Feeling you was like heaven, baby. Then I woke up, and you were sitting on my chest."

"That's right I was." I slid my hand underneath his tee shirt and felt the hard muscles of his abdomen; Dan loved working out, and I loved the results. "And I won't apologize for sitting on you, or all the salt I force fed you, or any of it. I needed you to come back to me."

"Always, baby," Dan said, then he fisted his hand in my hair, pulled my head back and kissed me. He wasn't usually rough, but I'd almost been seriously injured. The fact that I hadn't been was only due to this protection bubble we still didn't fully understand, but we would think about that later. Right now, I only needed him to keep kissing me.

Dan pulled off his shirt and then my towel, then he went to his knees and pushed my thighs apart. He licked me, long and slow and just hard enough, and my whole body shivered.

"On your back," I said, and he laid on the floor. Don't get me wrong, having Dan's mouth on me was amazing, but that wasn't what I wanted. I needed him inside me, more than I needed air or water or sunlight. I needed him.

I freed his cock and slid down onto him, and showed him just how much I needed him. I'd barely found my rhythm before my orgasm slammed into me, with Dan coming a moment later.

"I fucking love you," I said, as I laid against his chest. He was still mostly dressed, my hair was wet and cold, and we were lying on the hard wooden floor, and I'd never felt better in my life.

"I love you too, baby." Dan kissed the side of my head, and repositioned me in his arms. "This was almost a replay of what happened when we stayed at Andreas's place."

I hid my face against his neck, remembering how we'd brought food into our bed while we'd stayed in Andreas's downstairs apartment. It had been sticky, and messy, and so worth it. "I'm glad you didn't spread hummus all over me. But there's some honey in the kitchen," I added.

"Is there?" He squeezed my butt. "I know what I'm having for dessert."

Later, after we'd had a joint shower and reheated our dinner, we finished eating in the kitchen while Stuart whined for scraps. As I thumbed through my phone's calendar, I realized something.

"You know, if I'm thirteen weeks pregnant and Alicia's only eight weeks, the curse worked as intended," I said; a winter demon called Morozko had cursed Dan's generation of the Lyons family, so all the boys had to have children before the girls could. Quite odd as curses go, but we got past it. "Alicia must have gotten knocked up the first time Andreas nailed her."

Dan rubbed his eyes. "Can we never refer to my sister as having gotten nailed ever again?"

"She told me all about it," I continued, because Dan blushing was the cutest thing in the galaxy. "The term Greek god—"

"All right, I get it," he said. "Can't we just be happy for them and leave it at that?"

"I suppose." I dipped my toasty pita in tzatziki, ate the piece with the sauce, and fed the rest of the bread to Stuart.

"You never told her anything about us, did you?" he asked.

"Nah. I was trying to make a good impression." I fired off a text to Jill, then I got up to get something to drink. On my way to the fridge, I spied our rescued mandrake.

"Hey, our plant's looking good." I brought the plant to the table, and fluffed up the leaves.

"Think you can learn anything from it?" Dan asked.

"Hopefully," I said, then my phone beeped. I looked at it, and frowned.

"What's wrong?" Dan asked.

"The dead driver that hit the pillars? According to Jill, his name is Arthur Wexford."

"But Arthur Wexford was one of our victims."

"Yes. Also, Driver Arthur has been dead for months. He was wearing his funeral suit in the car."

"You mean to tell me a literal corpse was driving?" Dan demanded. "And he was a whole person, not a skeleton like Amir's dead army? Are zombies a thing? Be honest."

"I have never seen a fully fleshed corpse that's been dead for more than a few days reanimate," I replied. Based on his face, he did not appreciate that answer. "But more importantly, how many Arthur Wexford's are there?"

"Maybe it's a family name," Dan said. "The driver could have been the victim's father, or uncle."

"True." I glanced at Jill's message. "Jill's calling it a night. We'll know more tomorrow."

"Sounds like a plan." Dan poked at the mandrake. "So what does this guy do? Why do people think mandrakes equal witches?"

"It's used in flying ointment," I replied. "There's a recipe from a few hundred years ago that's been going around the internet for a while. Non-witches speculate if the ointment actually made witches fly, or if they just got really high and felt like they were floating."

"What do you think happened?"

"Not sure," I replied. "I've never made a flying ointment, therefore I have no first hand knowledge about how the concoction is supposed to work, and I'm not all that familiar with mandrake. However, I think actual flight would depend on the witch in question's power level. Levitation isn't an unusual talent."

"Can you levitate?"

"Obviously not. If I could do that, I wouldn't always be asking you to get things from the top shelves for me."

"Good point," Dan said, then he tossed Stuart a piece of grilled chicken. At this rate, Stuart was going to be the fattest dog in town. "Is the toxicity level of the plant what makes people high?"

"Exactly," I replied, impressed by his deduction. "You do listen to my ramblings."

"I'm always listening to you, baby." He got up and stretched, then he let Stuart out into the yard. "Let's clean up and head to bed. Tomorrow, first order of business is getting you in with the obstetrician. They we need to pick out a room, and start painting."

"Why do we need to paint?"

"The kid's room has got to be fun. No boring bedtimes in the Lyons house."

"Fun? Like a theme? Can we do dinosaurs?"

Dan wrapped his arm around me and kissed my hair. "Dinosaurs would be perfect."

Things Done in the Dark...

I began Friday morning by calling the medical center on the referral form we got from the hospital at eight sharp. By eight thirty, Eli had an appointment with an obstetrician set for Monday morning. That meant we could spend the rest of the day and the entire weekend working on the house, and getting it ready for our baby.

I could hardly believe we were having a baby.

"How much are we committing to the dinosaur theme?" Eli asked. We were on the second floor, standing in the room that would become the nursery. We picked the one that didn't have all my gym equipment in it, just to make our lives easier. "And where are we going to put all these boxes?"

"I will move those," I said, when Eli investigated one of them. The last thing I needed was her hauling crates up and down the stairs. "Honestly, I haven't looked in most of these in years. Most of it can probably go." I flicked open the cardboard flap on one of the boxes, and saw a collection of books I hadn't opened since college. "Maybe the library will want them."

Eli kissed my cheek. "Look at you, being generous." She went over to the window, and looked toward the senator's house on the hill. Now that I knew Barbara Stevens lived within sight of us, the conspiracy theorist in me kept coming up with wild scenarios. "I wonder when Barbara will want us to go over."

"Still floors me how well you two get along," I said. "She's not known for her warm personality."

"I inherited my dad's ability to get along with everyone," Eli said. "Besides, I rescued her kid."

I stood behind her, and wrapped my arms around her waist. "Yeah, you did," I said, as I nuzzled her neck. My hands drifted lower, then I felt a curve against her abdomen that hadn't been present before, and grinned.

"Got a little something going on here," I said, as I felt her small but present belly.

Eli twisted around in my arms, and said, "More than something, baby." I slid my hands down to her thighs and lifted her, fully prepared to take my beautiful wife back to bed and show her exactly how much I loved her. She'd just wrapped her legs around my waist when her phone buzzed.

"Back pocket," she said, as she unbuttoned my shirt. With one hand under her thigh, I retrieved her phone with the other. "You just wanted to touch my butt."

"You're the one that said back pocket," I said, as I handed her the phone. Eli hopped down, and frowned at the screen. "Is it about the case?" I asked.

"Sort of. Barbara wants to know if we want to head over to her place in a couple hours for lunch."

"Sure." I looked out of the window, and frowned at the senator's house. "Do you think it's weird that we were just staring at Barbara's house, then a minute later she texts you?"

"Hmm." Eli set her phone on the window sill, and followed my gaze. "As far as I know, Barbara has no supernatural abilities. If she's using magic, she hired someone to do it."

"Is that possible?"

"Most definitely. All those mentions of court magicians in the history books? Many of them were the real deal. Politicians and prime ministers still hire witches today."

I thought about the chaos surrounding the last big election. Magical involvement sure would explain a lot. "How do they get away with that?"

"It's a lot easier now, being that the general public doesn't believe in magic," she replied. "But back in the day, if you worked for the king, and you and the other court witches were keeping said king in power and his enemies at bay, you were pretty safe. And if the king got overthrown, you could always try to get in good with the new regime."

"That seems pretty harsh."

Eli shrugged. "It was what it was. For much of history, witches were just trying to survive, either by blending in or befriending people with power. Now, people think we're bedtime stories."

The way her voice caught at the end told me everything her words didn't. "Hey. Are you worried about our kid?"

She nodded, but wouldn't meet my eyes. "Yeah. I mean, not totally. I know we can keep him safe, but..." Eli turned toward the window, and dragged her hand across her cheek. "And now we've got these fake witches getting hung and a dozen mandrakes scattered beneath their feet, and..." She turned toward me, tears streaming down her face. "It's just scary, you know?"

I pulled her into my arms. "I know it is, baby," I said, as she sobbed against my chest. "I'm scared, too."

"Really?" Eli pulled back, and met my eyes. At the sight of her wide eyes and wet cheeks, my heart broke all over again. "Why are you scared?"

"The world's a scary place," I said, as I smoothed her hair back from her forehead. "I've seen some shit, just like you have. But I swear to you, Eliza Jayne, I will protect our kid with my life."

Eli smiled, and snuggled back into my arms. "I know you will. Our baby's going to be the safest kid in the galaxy."

I kissed the top of her head. "Safe as houses."

At eleven fifty-nine on the dot, Eli and I arrived at Senator Barbara Stevens's house. Barbara came from a certified New England political dynasty, and her home was set up more like a royal estate than a place where people actually lived. It had been in her family for years, and was used as a summer home by her great-grandfather, back when he was president. Yeah, her political roots ran deep, and she didn't let anyone forget it.

I wondered how the Stevens's wealth and power would stack up to something like the Allwood clan.

After we convinced the security detail we weren't criminals, we were ushered into the dining room. The senator was seated at the head of the table, with folders and stacks of paperwork spread out in front of her. When she saw Eli, she smiled.

"Eliza, Dan, thank you for coming," Barbara said, as she slipped into her party hostess role. "I hear congratulations are in order, Mr. and Mrs. Lyons! Why did you decide to have such a small ceremony?"

"We didn't want to make a big deal about getting married," Eli said, leaving off how we actually got married back in the seventeenth century by one of her ancestors. "We just wanted to be together."

Barbara clasped her hands together over her heart. "That's so romantic! And from Detective Lyons, who, as I recall, was all business."

"What can I say. I make exceptions for Eli. And I'm not on the force any longer," I added, since I didn't want anyone to assume we were there on official police business. "I'm in the private sector now."

"Well, the police certainly lost out on an excellent officer," Barbara said. "Sit, both of you. Lunch should be ready soon, and until then, we can talk about your case."

"Thanks," Eli said, as she glanced toward the staff milling around near the sideboard. Man, I hoped eggs weren't on the menu. "Have you heard anything about the case?"

"Only what's been reported on the news," Barbara replied. "Three people were found, is that right?"

"Exactly right," I said. "Our victims were found hanging in the park adjacent to City Hall. We're still waiting on a cause of death."

"You don't think hanging was the cause?" Barbara asked.

"My gut says otherwise," I replied.

"Can you think of any reason why someone would leave corpses at City Hall?" Eli asked. "I know the mayor's up for reelection, but I can't imagine anyone would commit murder for that."

"Oh, Eliza," Barbara said. "Politicians have done worse than dump bodies on the rivals' doorsteps to garner votes. But I do agree with you. I don't see how it would tie into the mayor's race."

"Is it correct that you endorsed the current mayor, Seamus Gove?" I asked.

Barbara pursed her lips. "Is your real question why I chose not to endorse my sister, Lillian?"

"The thought had crossed my mind."

"Well." Barbara poured three cups of coffee, and handed two of them to Eli and me. "First of all, Lillian has never held public office. She's never shown an interest in public service, yet now she wants to be mayor of the town we live in."

"She's quite a bit younger than you, right?" Eli asked. "Maybe it took her a while to figure out what she wanted to be when she grows up."

"Grow up? Lillian?" Barbara scoffed. "That will never, ever happen. I have no idea why she decided to run for mayor, but believe me, she wouldn't do the slightest bit of good for this town. Mayor Gove certainly isn't perfect, but he is the better choice."

"What is Lillian good at?" I asked. "Maybe she just needs a nudge in the right direction."

Barbara tapped her chin, and mimed thinking hard. "What is she good at? Let's see, not paying bills? Draining the liquor cabinet? Making an absolute spectacle of herself at the expense of our family?"

"She sounds like quite the handful," I said. "Does she live here, too?"

"She used to, but she moved out shortly after Abby was born. I couldn't have such a bad influence around my daughter."

"You made the right choice, because Abby is perfection," Eli said, and Barbara offered up a genuine smile. "How is my best girl?"

"Doing very well," Barbara replied. "She's in second grade now. Oh, excuse me. My assistant is trying to get my attention."

Barbara grabbed a folder, and walked to the far side of the room. Eli whipped out her phone and did some typing. When my phone pinged, I read the text she'd just sent me.

Eli: Check out her assistant. Be slick.

"I'm always slick," I grumbled, then I stood to grab the sugar bowl. As I did, I glanced over my shoulder, and almost choked.

The senator's assistant was none other than Megan Bergquist.

"What do we do?" Eli asked.

"Let's be direct," I said, then I turned around and waved at Megan. She went white as a sheet. "Nice to see you, Ms. Bergquist. I'm surprised you're working, what with the recent tragedy."

"You two know each other?" Barbara asked. "And what's this about a tragedy?"

Megan stared at me for a moment, then she said, "My sister passed recently."

"Oh, Megan, I'm so sorry to hear that," Barbara said. "Please, take some time off if you need to. Family comes first, always."

"I'm okay," Megan said, then she offered a weak smile to Barbara. "Really."

"I'm glad to hear that, but let me know if anything changes," Barbara said. "And how do you know Dan and Eli?"

"She hired us," I said, taking advantage of Megan's shocked-to-silence state. "Her sister was one of the people found behind City Hall."

Always Come to Light

After Dan's super smooth announcement, Barbara sent the rest of her staff home for the day, then the four of us sat down to talk. It soon became apparent that Barbara hadn't even known Megan had a sister.

"It's not that I was keeping anything about my family from you," Megan explained. "I just try not to mention my personal life at work."

"That's understandable," Barbara said. "How did you learn about Eliza and Dan's investigations business? Did you decide to hire them after Colleen was found?"

"When I heard about the bodies in the park, I was appalled, but I didn't think they had anything to do with me or my sister," Megan said. "However, it had been some time since I heard from Colleen. I went to Nine Lives Investigations to see if they could help me find her. I didn't know Colleen was dead until a police officer arrived at their house, and took my statement."

Barbara nodded, though she was frowning so hard a little line had formed between her eyebrows. "I still don't know why I'm just hearing about this now. I understand and respect your need for privacy, but having your sister found behind City Hall is something I think you'd mention."

"After I knew Colleen was gone—gone and dangling behind City Hall—all I could think about was how bad this would look for you," Megan said, red faced, though she seemed more upset at being found out than over her sister's demise. "Colleen had been using a fake name. I was hoping all of this would blow over and you'd never have to worry about it."

"Megan." Barbara leaned forward and set her hand on Megan's forearm. "Keeping secrets rarely ends well."

Megan nodded. "I know."

"When did you first decide to hire us?" I asked.

"That morning, right before I went to your place," she replied. "I called Colleen for the umpteenth time and it went straight to voice mail, and she hadn't responded to my emails for weeks. That was the last straw."

"But why us?" I pressed.

"I told you then, I went to you because you deal with weird cases."

I glanced at Dan, and said, "Yeah, you said that, and at the time we accepted that claim at face value. But now we're all sitting here in Barbara's dining room, and you're her assistant, and these coincidences are stacking up." I leaned forward, and asked, "Are you going to tell me you didn't know I was the one that found Abby after she was taken?"

Megan swallowed, and looked at her hands. "I knew. I mean, everyone knows how you're the big hero who rescued the senator's kid."

"I am not a hero," I said, as I shook my head. "I was just in the right place at the right time."

Megan nodded, but remained silent. I looked at Dan, and shrugged.

"Before we go any further," he began, "I want to make it clear that this is not an interrogation. Eli and I aren't cops. We're all on your side, and we want to find out what happened to Colleen."

"I appreciate that," Megan mumbled.

"Ms. Bergquist, I really want to believe you," he said. "I have three sisters of my own, and I would be devastated if anything happened to them. But you've got to admit, this is all looking a little odd. Is there anything else you think we should know about Colleen? Anything that you think might help us figure out what happened to her?"

"I-I can't think of anything," Megan said.

"Do you know a Jerry Goldman or Arthur Wexford?" I asked.

"Jerry Goldman?" Barbara repeated. "That's my accountant's name. Why did you mention him?"

"Barbara. Those are the names of the victims found alongside Colleen."

Barbara went white as a sheet. "Oh. All right. Let me make a call." She stood, and withdrew her phone as she stepped out of the room. I turned to Megan and smiled.

"I know this is freaky," I said to her, "but take it from the queen of the weird cases. If you follow the facts, anything can be solved."

"Follow the facts, and follow money," Dan said. "The bad guys need funds, and since most companies don't hire criminals, they tend to leave behind a pretty wide financial trail. You've just got to uncover it, and follow the clues."

"You make it sound so simple," Megan said. "Did you guys check out that magic shop? The one you said Colleen was going to?"

"Oh, yeah," I replied. "That place is creep central."

Barbara reentered the room, and leaned on the sideboard. "I've just had confirmation that Jerry is gone. That was my accountant hanging from the oak behind City Hall," she said.

"I am so sorry, Barbara," I said. "Is there anything I can do for you?"

"I think it's more about what I can do for you," Barbara said. "Two out of three victims are associated with me. My sister is running for mayor. This case of yours has something to do with me, or my family."

I didn't want to agree with her, but as Dan would say, the clues were stacking up. "Can you think of anyone who has it out for you?"

Barbara scoffed. "That's a long list. What was the third person's name?"

"Arthur Wexford," Dan said. "Interestingly enough, Eli and I were involved in a traffic accident yesterday. A completely different Arthur Wexford was the man behind the wheel."

"Are you all right?" Megan asked.

"We're all good," I replied. "Also, a Francesca Wexford owns the magic shop. We believe she's Arthur's sister."

"Then this involves all of us," Barbara said. "What's the common denominator?"

"Abby," I said. "And witches."

"What do witches have to do with anything?" Barbara demanded. "This isn't a bedtime story, Eliza. And how do these people know anything about Abby?"

"Colleen fell in with a bunch of witch hunters, for one," I said. "And you, me, and Dan know each other because of Abby's kidnapping."

"Where is Abby?" Dan asked. "Is she safe?"

"She's at school." Barbara checked her phone. "Her location confirms she's still there."

"We should have Jill run the victims against the people convicted of Abby's kidnapping," I said. "We need to rule out any associations."

"You think my sister wanted to kidnap someone?" Megan demanded.

"No, but if she heard about such a plot and tried to stop it, that's probable cause for murder," Dan said. "Have you ever met Goldman?"

"Maybe once or twice," Megan replied. "He only came by to pick up ledgers and receipts, and it wasn't often. We keep almost everything on spreadsheets now."

Follow the money. "How long had Jerry worked for you?" I asked Barbara.

"A few years," she replied. "And to answer your next question, I haven't noticed any money missing, but if I may sound like an out of touch rich lady for a moment, there's a lot of money tied up in our assets. He could have skimmed funds for decades before we noticed."

"We'll get a forensic accountant to review the books," Dan said. "I'll call Officer Sanders, and fill her in on what we've learned today. I'm sure it will help her investigation."

"Thank you, Dan," Barbara said. "I have to say, when Eliza reached out to me, I wasn't expecting to have such a strong connection to this case."

"Neither were we," I said. "But I sent you that text on a hunch. Sometimes, our intuition points us where we need to go."

Megan bit her lip. "Do you think it will point you toward whoever hurt my sister?"

"I've got a feeling it will."

Mandrake and Foresight

"I think I should summon Colleen's spirit to my grandmother's house," I said. Dan and I had left Barbara's house a few minutes ago, and we were on our way home. Or rather, we were going home, until I announced an unplanned detour.

"Oh?" Dan asked. "Why is that?"

"I'm not sure," I admitted. "But my foresight wants us at Gran's."

"Then we'll go there," Dan said, as he pulled into a parking lot to turn around.

"Wait," I said. "Let's go home and grab the mandrake!"

"Okay." Dan looked both ways, and pulled back onto the road in the same direction we'd been traveling. "Is there a particular reason why we're inviting mandrake to the party?"

"I'm not sure about that, either," I said. "But it will help. Really."

"You don't need to convince me. Your foresight's always right, even if it's a little crazy sometimes," he added, as he flashed me a smile. "But do me a favor, and ask it if we need to pick up anything else. I'd like to avoid unnecessary u-turns."

My foresight stayed quiet for the rest of the ride, even when I sent a text to my father letting him know we'd be stopping by. He replied pretty quickly and told me that him and Tessa were out running a few errands. When we arrived at Gran's, it was just me, Dan, and the mandrake. Oh, and the cats.

The cats—Pumpkin, Smokey, and Muffaletta—were once thought to be the ghosts of my grandmother's childhood pets. However, through a series of supernatural events, we now knew that they were the guardians of the power nexus that hovered above Gran's house. While the cats were awesome, on that day I was much more interested in the nexus.

Being that I'm the Mistress of Seers, I never need a power boost in order to summon a spirit, no matter how long ago the person in question had moved on. But weird things had been happening ever since Jill called us to consult on this very weird case, and the nexus offered an extra degree of protection from anything that might harm us. Right now, I needed all the protection I could get.

"What if the nexus amplifies Colleen's spirit a little too much?" Dan asked, as we settled around the kitchen table. Pumpkin was draped across my shoulders while the other two cats vied for Dan's attention. He set the mandrake on the counter, and scooped up both of the cats in his arms. "Will she end up like Jacob, almost alive?"

"As much as I don't want her to be dead, I don't think that would be a good thing," I said. "Everyone already knows she's gone. If her spirit starts wandering around town, that will entail a lot of explaining, especially if she's only corporeal for a short time. And imagine how Megan would react! We don't need to add to her stress, or anyone else's."

"Yeah, we're all stressed enough as it is." Dan went into the pantry, and emerged with a few plain white pillar candles. "Will three candles be enough?"

"Should be." I set Pumpkin on the table, and said to her, "We're going to summon a ghost, who may or may not be a good person. I need you to keep an eye out for anything weird. Can you help me?"

Pumpkin set her paw on my cheek, then she jumped off the table and summoned the other two to her side. They circled each other for a moment, then they jumped onto the counter and arranged themselves into a perfect line facing us.

"The muscle is in place," Dan said. "Ready?"

"Might as well do it now." I snapped my fingers, and the candle wicks ignited. "Colleen Bergquist," I called out, as I motioned for Dan to turn off the lights. It was a lot easier to see ghosts in a darkened room, without direct light washing them out. "I'd like to talk to you, if you have a moment."

"It's not like I have anything else to do," Colleen said, as she materialized near the solarium's door. "You're the one that talks to dead people?"

"Obviously. I'm Eliza, but my friends call me Eli. This is Dan."

Colleen looked from me to Dan. "Why are you calling me now? I've been dead for days. Maybe weeks, by now."

"I'm sorry to hear that," Dan said. "Would you mind telling us the last thing you remember?"

"I'm not sure," Colleen replied. "Whenever I try to figure out what happened, everything gets fuzzy."

Dan nodded, then he asked, "How did you know about Eliza?"

"Know what?" Colleen demanded.

"You said I'm the one who talks to dead people," I said. "Where did you learn that?"

"The rumors are that there's a secret group of people in town who talk to the dead," Colleen replied. "They said you were an old lady, though, like a magic grandma."

I glanced at Dan and he nodded; whoever was disseminating this information must have been referencing my grandmother, Helena Moore. She was Mistress of Seers for more than a century, but she'd been gone for almost five years.

"Sorry to say, but your information is a little outdated," I said. "We were hired by Megan. She was devastated to hear that you'd passed."

Colleen snorted. "I bet. She only called me to tell me where not to be, so I didn't accidentally run into her and ruin her perfect cookie cutter image. Is she still trailing after the bitch senator?"

"You mean Senator Stevens?" Dan asked. "Megan's her assistant. Did you know anyone else who worked for the senator?"

"No," Colleen replied. "Politics aren't my thing, even though I'm surrounded by it."

While Dan made some notes, I asked, "You were found alongside two men. Do you remember anything about that?"

"I was found," Colleen began, then her eyes widened. "I was found with two men? Was I... Did they do something to me?"

"We're not sure," I said. "When I was at the scene, your body was fully clothed."

Colleen stared at me for a moment, then looked away. "That's good, I guess. Hey, you have a mandrake."

"I do," I said. "I dug it up near where you were found."

"That's funny. My friend just bought a bunch of mandrake so we could... I can't remember why she wanted it. The lore says mandrake grows beneath a..." Colleen whirled around to face me. "I was hanged?"

"Yes," I said. "I'm so sorry."

"Yeah," Collen said, as she faded from view. "Me, too." In another moment, she was gone.

"That was not what I expected," I said, as Dan snuffed the candles. "She didn't seem to know how she died."

"You believe her?"

"She really has no reason to lie." I touched the mandrake's leaves. "And she recognized this plant. Because her friend bought a bunch..."

"And that friend just might be Lillian Stevens," Dan finished. "Although, we don't know why she wanted them."

"I wonder where she got the plants," I murmured, as I scratched Smokey's ears. "I think we need to look into Megan, and Lillian."

"The other two victims, too," Dan said. "What if they used aliases like she did? Colleen might know them under another name."

"Just like how others knew her as Shyla Nae," I said, referencing Colleen's tarot card alter ego. "Should we start with bringing Jill up to speed?"

"Sure." Dan took out his phone and started typing. "What are you going to work on?"

"I am going to talk to the mandrake."

Communicating with the mandrake wasn't particularly enlightening, but it was relaxing.

While Dan discussed the case and persons of interest with Jill, I sat in the solarium with our guest of honor. Most of the plants in the solarium were poisonous, so I figured the mandrake would fit right in. As ever, the cats were lounging in a ring around me. A casual observer would think they were napping, but not me. They'd formed a perimeter, and wouldn't let anyone near me they didn't approve of. We didn't call them the Feline Federation for nothing.

Dan entered the solarium and sat next to me on the chaise. The cats didn't even twitch a whisker, further proof that the little traitors liked him more than me.

"Talking with Jill is exhausting," Dan said. "How did I ever make it as a cop?"

"You were a damn good cop, and you know it," I said. "Did you learn anything useful?"

"Yes and no," he replied. "Jill didn't know that Goldman worked for the senator, so that was good information for her. And, I got confirmation that the hanging Arthur Wexford was the corrections officer that got fired because of his relationship with Cecily."

"That's progress," I said. "Any updates on driving Arthur Wexford?"

"Preliminary information states that he's an uncle that passed around a year ago, but the coroner won't sign off on that report for obvious reasons," Dan replied. "But the body didn't have any signs of trauma beyond what you'd expect in an auto accident. Jill said it was like someone put Arthur's corpse in the car and sent it careening into the pillars."

"But how did the car manage to hit the pillars?" I shook my head. "Making a car move forward with magic is easy. Controlling it through traffic and making it hit a specific target is very difficult, and would require a direct line of sight."

"And the magic shop is right across the street," Dan concluded. "Babe, that shop is bad news. What do you think's gonna happen when we go to that bookstore tomorrow?"

I tugged at the mandrake's leaves. "I wish I knew."

"Me, too." Dan wrapped his arm around me, and kissed my hair. "Have you learned anything, either from Mr. Plant or your foresight?"

"The plant is happy to be watered and out of the cold," I replied. "As for my foresight, it's being rather quiet. However, I don't think Barbara's involved in whatever this is. She seems to be the victim here."

I sat straight up and faced Dan. "That! That was my foresight. Barbara's the victim!"

"All right," he said. "Let's figure out who would deploy magic against a senator."

We began our research by looking into Lillian's social media accounts. Hoo boy, that girl was a party animal.

"Here she is in Costa Rica last fall, and before that she had a sojourn to Ibiza," Dan said, as he scrolled through pictures Lillian had posted on her public pages. Every single image showed her laughing and having an apparent great time.

"From what I can gather, it seems like she came home from South America, and the next day decided to run for mayor."

"That tracks with what Barbara said," I mumbled, as I pulled the property records for Lillian's house. "But why is she running?"

Dan shrugged. "Maybe she wants to make a difference?"

"But still. Why now?" I glanced over my notes, and continued, "Lillian is twenty-eight years old and has never worked a day in her life. Her house is owned by her family trust, and all her expenses are taken care of. Then she makes a complete one-eighty and decides to go into public service?" I tapped my pencil against my notebook as if the action could summon answers. Sadly, it didn't. "Something happened to change her attitude so drastically."

"I agree," Dan said. "Have you ever met her?"

"No. Barbara is not a fan of her sibling, so she's never been around when I was over at her place." I dropped my pencil and stretched. "Have you ever met the current mayor?"

"Seamus Gove? Yeah, I've met him a few times," Dan replied. "He made a point of attending every police function he could. He's a strong believer in public service."

"Is he a good guy? Like, would you invite him to our house?"

"Not sure if I'd invite him over for dinner," Dan admitted. "But I'd grab a beer with him. He's never come off as untrustworthy, or that he was anything but a humble guy looking out for the city."

"Hmm. Maybe we should interview him about the bodies. The investigation can be our in, then we can ask him about the upcoming election."

"Actually, let me ask Jill if anyone's interviewed him already," Dan said, as he sent Jill a message. "I really don't want you going near City Hall or that magic shop unless it's absolutely necessary."

I opened my mouth to protest, but Dan was right. If someone was willing to throw a whole car at us, who knew what else they would do. "Okay. If we can't talk to Gove, how can we talk to Lillian?"

"Good question. Do we know anyone she knows, other than Barbara?"

"That's a great question." I scrolled through her pictures again. "None of these people look familiar to me."

"Maybe we can reach out as concerned citizens, and interview her about the homicides," Dan suggested. "Politicians love free advertising. She could repurpose that interview a hundred different ways."

"I don't like the idea of my casework being repurposed," I mumbled. "What if the actual killer got a hold of it, and used it against us? There has to be another way."

Dan's phone vibrated. "Jill said she will reach out to Gove, and bring us in as consultants. She's pretty confident she can make the interview happen."

"That's good," I said, as I scrolled through the pictures of Lillian frolicking on tropical beaches and guzzling drinks decorated with tiny umbrellas for the umpteenth time. "Do you think it's weird that she still has her party girl persona out on social media? One would think she'd scrub these images so she appeared serious about running, and yet."

"Maybe she isn't serious," Dan said. "Barbara told us that Lillian has never been serious about anything. What if she doesn't really want to be mayor?"

"Then why bother with a campaign," I began, then my foresight sparked. "She's doing this to discredit her sister. Remember, Barbara is the victim." I scrolled back to Lillian's campaign website and clicked on the email form. "I'm contacting her campaign about us interviewing her. I need to be in the same room with Lillian so my foresight can get a read on her."

"What if it reads something bad?" Dan asks. "Or magical?"

I sighed, or maybe that was just my brain leaking. This case was taking everything I had, and I felt like for every tiny step forward we made, we got pushed two steps back. "I suppose we'll figure that out when it happens."

A LITTLE AWKWARD

Saturday morning started out with a bang. I woke up next to the most beautiful woman in the world, walked the dog, then I made breakfast. We'd just sat down to eat our pancakes when my phone rang. I accepted the call, and barked, "Lyons."

"Dan," Eli whispered. "You're going to scare them."

I grinned, because some people needed a good scare now and then. "Sorry, Nine Lives Investigations."

"Hi, is this Dan?"

"Sure is. What can I do for you?"

"This is Dahlia, from The Black Hat. You offered to give people a ride to the bookstore this morning?"

"Hey, Dahlia. Yeah, I remember the stakeout," I said, as I gestured to Eli for a pen and paper. She waved her fork at me and kept eating. "Who are we picking up?"

"Me, if that's okay."

"Of course it is. Text me the address, and we'll be there in about an hour."

"Thanks, Dan!"

I ended the call, and looked at Eli. "I was asking for something to write with."

My phone vibrated with an incoming text. Eli glanced at the screen, and said, "Looks like you've got it covered. That Dahlia's address?"

"Yes, ma'am. She called looking for a ride. Still up for the bookstore?"

"Why not? While we're there, we can get more coffee."

As promised, an hour later, my overly caffeinated wife and I pulled up in front of Dahlia's place. She rented an apartment in one of the old Victorian homes that had been converted into multi-family dwellings a few decades back, and it was in a nicer part of town. Actually, it was only a block away from Eli's grandmother's house.

"Interesting location," I said, as we waited out front.

"Yes, it is," Eli said, as she faced the direction of her grandmother's place. "Remind me to tell Tess."

"Will do," I said, then Dahlia exited from the front door and waved. We waved back, and she let herself into the back seat.

"Thanks so much for giving me a ride," Dahlia said, as she buckled up. "Do you need directions to the bookstore?"

"I know where it is," I replied, as I pulled away from the curb.

"Dan has a mental map of the city," Eli added. "Sometimes I think that when he was a cop, all he did was drive around memorizing the street signs."

"Knowing your assigned territory is a smart move," I said.

"Why did you leave the police force?" Dahlia asked. "If you don't mind my asking."

"I don't mind at all," I replied. "Basically, the chief and I got in an argument, he suspended me, and I never went back. That's the entire, boring story."

"And you were never a police officer?" Dahlia asked Eli.

"Oh, no," Eli replied. "I've really only ever worked for myself, or my family. I went into investigations because I'm good at puzzles."

"That's great, that you knew what you wanted to do," Dahlia said. "I've only ever had retail jobs."

"Retail work is good work," Eli said.

"I thought you were into the whole magic shop life," I said. "Herbs and candles and keeping the mortals safe."

"I am." Dahlia met my gaze in the rearview mirror, then looked out the side window. "It just gets a little weird sometimes, you know?"

"I bet," Eli said. "All that stuff Francesca said the other day spooked me a bit."

Dahlia's head snapped toward Eli. "How do you know her name? I only introduced her as the owner. She doesn't like it when people know her name," she added, a bit panicked.

"I pulled the property records," Eli said. "Old PI habit. I won't mention her name to anyone."

"Oh, good," Dahlia said. Her relief was palpable, and interesting.

"Would you get in trouble if Francesca thought you told us her name?" I asked.

"No, it's not that," Dahlia said. "It would just be a little awkward, you know?"

"Yeah." I knew one thing for sure, and it was that Dahlia was scared of her employer. I made a mental note to discuss that with Eli later on, then I parked behind the bookstore. "We have arrived."

"We're probably going to see some people from the gathering the other day," Dahlia said as we walked toward the store. "Don't say hi or interact with anyone. We're supposed to keep to ourselves and observe."

"Fine by me," Eli said. "I'm only here for the coffee. And maybe a few baked goods," she added, as she grinned at Dahlia. "Ready?"

"Ready," Dahlia replied, and I held the door open for them. "I hope they have chocolate muffins, too."

"I'm going to check out the bookstore," I said, since Eli and Dahlia were getting along so well. "Get me a black coffee, please."

"Okay," Eli said, then she walked toward the café. I watched her walk away for a moment, then I turned toward the shelves.

The bookstore was best described as organized chaos. The shelves near the front were meticulously put together, and filled with flashy art books and impulse purchases like journals and colorful pens. However, when you ventured deeper into the store, piles of books were stacked haphazardly on tables, shelves, and even a few chairs. Everything was still roughly organized by subject, and the selection was amazing, especially on the second hand side of the place. This pace was a book lover's dream. I was working my way through a stack of vintage science fiction magazines when I heard a familiar voice.

"Well, hello there," Bennet said, as he emerged from the nonfiction section with an armload of books. I glanced at the spines, and saw that they were all about plants in one way or another. "I didn't expect to see you here this morning."

"Likewise," I said, as we shook hands. "What's with the books? I thought you already knew everything about plants."

"If only," Bennet said. "Care to join me in the café?"

"Sure. Eli's over there with one of her friends."

"Excellent," Bennet said. "We can order a pot of tea for the table. I believe today's scone flavors are bacon cheddar and coconut raspberry."

"Wouldn't want to miss that." I grabbed a few magazines, and after we paid for our reading material, Bennet and I entered the café. It was larger than the bookstore side of the business, and it was packed. Of course, all of these people were from The Black Hat and on an actual witch hunt, but hopefully that would be over soon. The only witch in the place was Eli, and no one suspected her.

Or did they?

At the thought of my wife being set up by this group, cold sweat broke out on the back of my neck. Frantically, I scanned the crowd. I found Eli standing on the far side of the café. She and Dahlia were checking out a display of tea and fancy boxed chocolates. Leaving Bennet to find a table on his own, I made a beeline toward her.

"Babe," I said, as I put my hand on Eli's elbow. Being in contact with her calmed my racing heart. "Everything okay in here?"

"Yes, Mr. Over Protective," she replied, as she handed me my coffee. "Check out all the chocolate varieties!"

"That's certainly a lot," I said, as I glanced at the gold and pink ribboned boxes. "Bennet's here. He said the scone flavors are bacon cheddar and coconut something."

"Coconut is a definite no," she said, which gave me hope for the other flavor. I could use more bacon in my life. "Where's Bennet?"

"He's right over—"

I turned around, and stopped dead. Every single person in the café was glaring at Bennet as if he was the actual devil. Everyone, except me, Eli, and the people working behind the counter.

"Eli," Dahlia hissed, as she grabbed my wife's arm. "There he is! That's the man who's suspected of using magic!"

Eli followed Dahlia's gaze, and gasped. The crazed witch hunters were after Bennet.

Light the Torches

"That man?" I asked Dahlia, as I watched Bennet read over the café's menu. For the first time in my life I wished I had telepathy instead of foresight, so I could tell Bennet to get the hell out of there. "He's no magician. He works at the local college in the horticulture department. Basically, he's a fancy gardener."

"Wait, you know him?" Dahlia demanded.

"Yeah. His name is Bennet. He knew my grandmother." I tugged Dahlia toward Bennet's table. It was like tugging on a statue. "Come on, I'll introduce you. He's super nice. Promise."

Dahlia nodded, and we walked toward Bennet's table. Dan followed close behind us, while keeping an eye on the rest of the café.

"Hey, Bennet," I said. "This seat taken?"

"Hello, Eli, and hello again, Dan," Bennet said, as the three of us sat around the table. "I was surprised to see Dan in the stacks. I didn't know you frequented this café."

"This is the first time I've been here in a while," I said. "Bennet, this is my friend Dahlia. I was just telling her how you're a fancy gardener."

"Ah, well," Bennet said, as he got flustered in that quintessentially British way of his. "I don't know if anything I do could be called fancy. More often than not, I'm up to my elbows in dirt."

"Gotta do the work if you want the results," Dan said. He was casually lounging in his chair while he watched the rest of the café with his sharp detective's gaze. Nothing got past Dan, not even the smallest detail.

"Isn't that the truth," Bennet said. "Dahlia, what do you do for work?"

"I, uh, work the register at The Black Hat," she replied. "It's a new store downtown."

"Oh? Do you have an interest in haberdashery?" Bennet asked.

"They don't sell hats," I said. "It's a magic shop."

"Ah, so the shop's name references the top hat from which a stage musician liberates a rabbit," Bennet deduced, and Dahlia giggled.

"I never thought of it like that," she said. "Eli told me that you know her grandma?"

"Knew," Bennet amended. "Helena passed on some years ago."

Dahlia turned to me. "I'm so sorry."

"Thank you," I said. "But yeah, Gran and Bennet go way back."

"Really." Dahlia eyed Bennet over the rim of her coffee mug. "You don't look old enough to hang with grandmas. All that gardening must keep you in shape."

Bennet positively beamed at that. I nudged Dan's leg with my foot, because holy cow, Dahlia had gone from being scared of Bennet to shamelessly flirting with him in the blink of an eye, but he didn't acknowledge me. I nudged him a bit harder, and finally got his attention. He looked at me, then he stood up.

"We're leaving," Dan announced. "Bennet, come with us."

"I haven't yet ordered my tea," he protested.

"We'll get you some tea somewhere else." Dan grabbed the magazines he'd purchased, and stood over us like a bodyguard. That was when I realized that everyone in the café was staring at us, and they looked angry.

"Come on, Bennet," I said, as I got up and shouldered my bag. "They're a second away from lighting the torches. Did you drive here?"

"No, I walked," Bennet replied.

"What about me?" Dahlia asked.

"Are you part of this witch hunt?" Dan demanded. "Because if you are, you can stay away from us."

"It's not a witch hunt," Dahlia began, then Ron, the man we'd met at the gathering in the magic shop's basement who'd asked us an awful lot of question about our cases, took a step toward Dan. A few other men flanked him, and they stared us down.

"Face it, Dahlia, the hunt's on," I said. "Make your choice because we're leaving now."

I looped my arm with Bennet's and we made a beeline toward the door. Dan kept his hand on my elbow the entire time, until he opened and held the door for us. As soon as I stepped outside, I exhaled, thinking we were in the clear.

I was wrong.

"Dahlia," Ron yelled. I turned, and saw that Dahlia had followed us outside. Good for her.

"Yeah, Ron?" she asked.

"You sure you want to leave with these sorts?" he demanded.

"Have to," Dahlia replied. "They're my ride."

"I can take you home."

"No, thank you," Dahlia said. "See you around."

"It's no trouble," Ron said, as he closed the distance between him and Dahlia. He stopped short when Dan stepped between them.

"She said no," Dan said. "Where I come from, when a lady says no, a gentleman accepts that answer."

"Where you come from?" Ron sneered. "Is that another bullshit story about your time as a cop? I know for a fact that the force doesn't hire witches!"

"Is that so? Being that I am not a witch, I wouldn't know either way," Dan said, then he turned to usher us toward the SUV. "We're leaving. Have a good day."

"I didn't say you could go," Ron said, then he made the biggest mistake of his life and clamped his hand onto Dan's shoulder.

Faster than my eyes could follow, Dan got out from under Ron's hand and twisted his arm behind his back. "Just so you know, I was a cop," Dan said, as Ron tried to squirm away. He didn't have any luck, since Dan's arms were like steel bands. "Thirteen years I was on the force, both in Queens and right here in this town. All that time I spent in public service means I have plenty of experience dealing with bigots like yourself."

"I'm not a bigot," Ron protested. "Witches are evil!"

"What are you going to do when you find one?" Dan demanded. "Drop a house on them?"

"We'll stop them!"

"How?" Dan demanded. "Because murder is illegal, buddy."

"We wouldn't kill anyone," Ron said. "We would just make them leave."

"Just a little fear and intimidation." Dan released him, and Ron went flailing into last week's dirty snowbank. "Here's a word of advice, pal. A few days ago, someone strung up three people who were supposed to be witches behind City Hall, but guess what? There were just regular people like you and me."

"Witches need to—"

"Live a long, healthy life without fear of persecution?" I finished for him. "And, dumbass, those people weren't witches. Get it through your thick head."

"Let's go," Dan said. "Ron, buddy, don't you dare follow us, come after us, or even think about us ever again. I've got plenty of friends on and off the force."

Dan turned on his heel and herded us toward the truck. Ron watched us the entire time, but he didn't get up.

"You're sexy when you're mean," I said, once we were all buckled in.

"Eliza," Dan said. "Being sexy is not the goal here."

"Thank heavens for that," Bennet muttered.

I pulled down the sun visor and angled the mirror so I could see Dahlia. "Are you okay? That was pretty intense."

"I'm fine," Dahlia said. "This is the first time I've gone on one of those stakeouts. I didn't really think it would be like that. Thanks for getting us out of there, Dan."

"No problem," Dan said. "I protect and serve, even as a civilian."

A beep sounded from Bennet's chest pocket. "Oh, Lillian's calling," he said, when he checked the screen. "We're supposed to meet up later today. I'll tell her... Well, something."

My foresight sparked. "Lillian who?"

"Lillian Stevens," Bennet replied. "We've been getting to know each other."

My jaw dropped. "You're dating the senator's sister?"

"I don't know if we're dating," Bennet began, but Dan had had enough.

"The coincidences are piling up on this case, and I'm liking it less every second," Dan said. "We all need to sit down and have a very honest chat."

"We should go to Gran's," I said. "The house is warded, so if Ron and the goon squad follow us, we'll have extra protection. Besides, Tessa can kick all their asses."

"Who's Tessa?" Dahlia asked.

I twisted around in my seat. "Here's the thing. Bennet is not a witch. That's the truth. However, I am both a witch and a seer, and we're currently working a case where someone—perhaps a serial killer—is targeting suspected witches. We think the people hanging around your store are somehow involved. Now, if you want to wash your hands of all this, I wouldn't blame you. Say the word and we'll bring you straight home and you'll never see us again."

Dahlia pursed her lips, and looked down at her hands. "And what if I want to help?"

"Then we'd love to have you," I said. "Does that mean you're coming with us?"

"Yeah. I want to help you guys fix this mess. One question, though. Is Tessa a witch?"

"Is she ever."

Whiskey Before Noon

Since Gran's house was the safest place in town, that was exactly where we went. We got there just as my father was taking a batch of cinnamon rolls out of the oven.

"We didn't mean to disturb you," I began, worried we'd intruded on him and Tessa having a romantic morning.

"It's no bother," Dad said. "We have plenty for everyone. Isa just made fresh coffee, too. Bennet, do you still prefer Darjeeling?"

"If it's not too much trouble," Bennet replied.

"You know it's not," Dad replied, then he turned to Dahlia. "Hello. I'm Alex. Would you like some coffee, or tea?"

"I'm Dahlia, and I'm okay with just water," Dahlia said. "Are you Eli's brother, or something?"

Dad smiled. "I'm her father. Eli, would you please grab your friend a bottled water from the fridge?"

"Sure," I said, as I retrieved the water in question. "Where's Tessa?"

"She'll be down soon," he replied. "What brought the four of you here today?"

"If it's okay with you, I'll tell you once Tessa's here," I replied. "That way, I only have to tell the story once, and it's a doozy."

"Oh, so it's that sort of a visit." My father opened the cupboard above the stove and retrieved a large green glass bottle. "Dan, I was saving this for when the baby's born, but perhaps we'll need to open it today."

"What is it?" I asked, as I peeked over Dan's shoulder. "Wine?"

"It's a forty-year-old bottle of Scotch," a grinning Dan replied. "Alex, thank you so much. Wait, is this so we'll name the baby after you?"

Dad affected a shocked face. "You mean you weren't already going to name him after me? Alexander the Second has such a nice ring to it."

"Nice try," I said, as I sat at the table. "And I'm the one you need to be bribing for naming rights."

My dad laughed, and set about serving cinnamon rolls. He put two on my plate, which was a good starter bribe. Dahlia sat beside me, and whispered, "Are you pregnant?"

"Thirteen weeks," I replied. "Had an ultrasound to prove it."

"Congratulations," she murmured. "Is it safe for you to be doing... this?" she asked, as she gestured to encompass the entire room.

"I don't see why not." Pumpkin jumped onto my lap, and I rubbed her ears. "Witches and seers have been reproducing from the beginning. I'm sure me and the baby will be fine."

Dahlia frowned, but she didn't question me further. That was just as well, since Tessa picked that moment to make her grand entrance. As usual, she was dressed like a golden age Hollywood starlet, with her black hair swept up in an elaborate coif, and a red silk dress and matching heels. Why anyone would wear heels on a Saturday morning was beyond me.

"Whiskey before noon," Tessa said, when she saw the bottle of Scotch sitting on the table. "This is my kind of party. What are we celebrating?"

"This is more of a warning, and a plea for assistance," I said. "Sorry."

Tessa sighed, then she swiped a finger's worth of frosting from my dad's cinnamon roll. "Let's hear it."

Within an hour, Dan and I had filled my father and Tessa in on our case, the car accident, and Senator Stevens's ties to everything. We also learned that Bennet met Lillian a few weeks ago at the same café we'd been at that morning, and had gotten together with her every Saturday since then. However, what was most interesting was why The Black Hat's goon squad had targeted Bennet in the first place.

"It's because you grow magical plants," Dahlia explained; we'd also learned that she had just moved to town from Maine, and had only worked at The Black Hat for a few weeks. That meant she hadn't had time to be fully indoctrinated into the witch hunting cult. "Someone affiliated with the shop needed some of those plants, and you were the only person who could produce them."

"That's a pretty weak reason to call someone a witch," I said, as I nodded toward the solarium door. "Pretty much all plants have magical properties."

"No, this was a specific witchy plant," Dahlia said. "It had a weird name. Mandible?"

I stared at Dahlia for a moment, then I turned to Bennet. "Let me guess, you sold some kid from the student activities guild a bunch of mandrakes."

"Why, yes," Bennet replied. "I was approached in the fall about propagating a few specimens. I must say, the project was quite successful. I only set out to grow six plants, but I ended up with—"

"Fourteen," Dan and I finished in concert.

"How did you know that?" Bennet asked.

Dan withdrew his phone and pulled up the photos of our crime scene. "All fourteen of your plant babies ended up underneath our victims," he explained, as he showed Bennet the pictures. "Eli took one of them home, but the other thirteen are still there."

"Actually, the one I confiscated is in the solarium," I said. "I thought it might want to be with its baneful buddies."

"Curiouser and curiouser," Tessa said. "Bennet, do you have the name of the person who ordered these plants from you?"

"Yes, I do," he replied. "Her name was Megan Bergquist."

"Who is the sister of victim number two," Dan said. "This explains why she was so jittery when we saw her at Barbara's place."

"Jittery, but I don't think she killed anyone," I said. "At least, not directly. And one of the other victims was Jerry, who happens to be Barbara's accountant."

"This entire case is wrapped around the senator," Tessa said. "Especially when you add in Bennet's girlfriend."

"Lillian is not my girlfriend," Bennet protested. "But I must admit, it is odd how all of this is happening now, what with our recent acquaintance."

"This is all getting muddy, and what we need are some fresh eyes," Dan said, then he slid how phone toward Dahlia. "These are our three victims. Have you ever met or interacted with any of them?"

Dahlia touched Colleen's picture. "She was our tarot reader, Shyla Nae. Megan, the girl you mentioned. She's Shyla's sister?"

"That's right," I said. "Shyla's real name is Colleen."

Dahlia nodded, then she looked at Jerry's picture. "I've never seen this man, but I have seen the other one," she said, as she tapped Arthur Wexford's image. "He came into the shop looking for spells. Francesca took him into the back."

"Francesca is the shop's owner," I explained to the rest. "She also looks exactly like Cecily Allwood. Since we confirmed that Cecily is still in jail, we think it's a glamour."

"Glamours need a great deal of power to run efficiently," Tessa said. "Whoever this Francesca is, they're probably using some sort of an amplifier."

"What if she's powerful enough to sustain a glamour on her own?" Dan asked. "Could you do it, Tess?"

"Yes," she replied without hesitation. "But very few witches are as powerful as me, especially in this area."

"Do you have a list of these power players?" Dan asked. "We can cross them off, one by one."

"Jacob Allwood could do it," Tessa began, "but I doubt he'd create such a nonsense plan if he wanted to eliminate people. There's Eli's mother, but her powers are bound. That leaves..." Tessa looked at my dad, and frowned. "Nathaniel Beauclaire."

"Nathaniel being involved makes less sense than Jacob," I said. "He's crazy and powerful, but I don't think he'd bother with any of this. The last time we saw him, he was obsessed over Jemima's return." I glanced at Dahlia, and explained, "Jemima is Nathaniel's wife. Her spirit was trapped in a bottle."

"Like a genie," Dahlia murmured. "What if she got out?"

"What if, indeed," my father said. "But as interesting as that would be, it is unlikely. Firstly, someone would need to let her spirit out, which would most likely result in her moving on to the next realm. I don't think Nathaniel would risk losing her. The only other living person who would be interested in Jemima is her mother, Sara, who's also dead." Dad sucked in a breath, as he remembered that Sara had passed on but was still hanging out on the mortal plane. "Is her spirit still inhabiting Jada's body?"

"That corpse must have disintegrated by now," I said. "Which means that Sara's spirit could be inside literally anyone."

"And Sara is definitely powerful enough to sustain a glamour on her own," Tessa said. "However, Sara is also very smart. I don't think she'd risk her situation by committing such a public murder."

"This brings us back to the magic shop," Dan said. "Jacob told us that the shop used to be in Westhampton. Dahlia, do you know why it relocated?"

"Francesca said it was in a bad area," Dahlia replied. "Too much of the wrong kind of magic. You see, she separates magic into good and bad, and witches are the bad guys."

"Aren't we always," Tessa murmured. "And who are the good ones?"

"Humans," Dahlia replied, then she frowned. "Only, aren't witches human, too?"

Tessa beamed. "Dahlia, my pet, you have just figured out in a few seconds what the patriarchy has ignored for thousands of years. Yes, we are all humans, but witches and seers are not mortal."

"Then you'll live forever?" Dahlia asked.

"Not exactly. We do live a very long time, but mortals can do that, as well. However, most mortals don't want to bother studying the magic arts, and they become jealous of our power." Tessa faced me. "My guess is that this Francesca Wexford is a very jealous mortal who can't be bothered to learn how to cast a proper spell. She should be easy enough to contain."

"Maybe for you, but we've got to get her legally," Dan said. "Remember, this is a homicide case with three victims. If Francesca caused their deaths, I want her rotting in a mortal prison for a very long time."

"Agreed," my father said. "If for no other reason than to assure the public that no actual witches are harming people. We've been tried in the court of public opinion too many times, and I don't want to see it happen again."

"All right, then we have a plan," I said. "We do a deep dive into Francesca's background, and figure out her motive and opportunity. Dahlia, we'll need your help on that."

"Of course," she said. "I'll do whatever I can."

"Awesome. Tess, if you could check in with your contacts and make sure no extraordinarily powerful witches have recently come to the area, that would be swell."

"I'll send out some feelers this evening," Tessa said.

"Double awesome. And, Bennet?"

"Yes?"

"Can you arrange a meeting between us and Lillian?" I asked. "Something's still not right about her, and I can't put my finger on it."

"Of course," he replied. "How does an afternoon tea sound?"

"As long as I can have coffee instead, it sounds great."

THE MURDER HOUSE

This case was rapidly spiraling out of control, so Eli and I resorted to a tried-and-true tactic: divide and conquer.

Bennet set up an afternoon tea—which I didn't even know was a thing in this country—with Lillian Stevens for later that day, and Eli was going along for the ride. That way, she could ask Lillian a few questions about the victims associated with her sister, the mighty senator. As for me, Dahlia and I would swing by The Black Hat's former location in Westhampton and try to figure out why Francesca, the store's owner, had wanted to leave the area. If we were lucky, we might even find some incriminating evidence, neighbors to talk to, or maybe even a printout of her diabolical plan or villain monologue. You never know.

The reason Dahlia was coming with me was simple: she knew where the location was and could give directions, but she didn't know the street names. Eli ran a search for property owned by Francesca Wexford in Westhampton, but she didn't get any results. Therefore, having Dahlia as my temporary copilot would make this trip easier. And after we'd scoped out the area, I would drop Dahlia at home, and meet up with Eli for the end of tea time. As plans went, it was pretty good.

So why did I feel like we were missing something?

"Are you sure about splitting up?" I asked Eli, before we left. We'd ducked into the solarium for a few minutes of alone time before we headed out. "We can all go together."

"If a bunch of people show up at the teahouse with Bennet, it might spook Lillian," she said. "I'm hoping I'll be able to win her over."

"You win everybody over," I said, and it was the truth. Eli had this thousand-watt smile that went straight to your heart and melted it like butter on a hot day. "Just wait until Barbara finds out you were hanging out with her sketchy sister."

Eli laughed, and hid her face against my chest. "We don't even know if she's sketchy. It could just be sibling rivalry with those two, like you and Frank Junior."

"There is no rivalry between me and my littlest brother," I said; Frank Junior was older than me, but he was also shorter. Like, five inches shorter. He hated that fact as much as I loved it. "Maybe I just can't stand being apart from you for a few hours."

She laughed again, a deep throaty laugh that reverberated deep in my chest, and I swear my heart skipped a beat. "Just wait until I'm the size of a house and constantly grumpy. You'll be sick of me by then."

"Never." I kissed her, slowly at first, but Eli deepened the kiss right away. By the time her hand fisted in the front of my shirt, I had to remind myself that her father was in the next room. "Looks like you're not sick of me yet, either."

"You're okay." She took my phone from my chest pocket and checked the battery. "Make sure you charge this in the car, and keep your location on. As soon as you're at the old store, text me."

"Yes, ma'am," I said. "I like it when you worry about me."

"You're the one going into possible danger. I'm just going to have tea and crumpets with Bennet." Eli laid her head on my shoulder as she slid the phone back into my pocket. "Just be careful, okay? I don't want to be a widow or a single parent."

I almost made a smart-ass remark, but it wasn't often Eli worried. "I will be, baby," I said, as I kissed her hair. "Just like you're gonna be careful, and in a couple hours, we'll be back together so we can go over what we learned."

"That's right," she said. "Just a couple hours."

Soon after me and Eli's talk in the solarium, Dahlia and I were in the truck and heading west toward The Black Hat's original location. It was an old storefront on the main road, which was the only road that held anything interesting in that town. Since it was a bit of a ride, I decided to make some small talk.

"What made you come down here from Maine?" I asked Dahlia. "The bustling nightlife?"

"Very funny. I want to enroll in the local art school, so I moved down to the area. Since I can't enroll until the fall, I went looking for a job the day after I moved in. When I got to The Black Hat, Francesca hired me on the spot," she explained. "That was about a month ago."

That answered a pretty big question for me, since I couldn't put together how a down to earth kid like Dahlia ended up working at a magic shop. "And this morning's stakeout was the first one you've gone on?"

"Yeah. I really didn't think it would be like that. I..." Dahlia paused. I glanced at her, saw her staring at her hands fidgeting in her lap. "I never thought I'd be associated with people like that. They really wanted to hurt Bennet!"

"Don't beat yourself up over it," I said. "As soon as you knew what they were like, you got out. You made the right call."

"Thanks," she mumbled. "Oh, the store's coming up. It's right after that funky red tobacco barn."

"All right." I slowed down, and looked for the store's parking lot. "Did you ever work at this location?"

"No. I just helped Francesca clear some boxes out of the storage room. Here it is."

I pulled into the gravel parking lot, and got a look at The Black Hat's former home. It was a small, freestanding structure with a large front window. It reminded me of a gas station, though there weren't any pumps present.

"I wonder what made Francesca choose this spot," I said, as I turned off the engine. "I'm going to walk the perimeter."

I got out of the truck, then I took a picture of the empty store and sent it to Eli. She sent back a heart, which warmed my own. I took a few more pictures, and sent them to Jill.

Dan: Know anything about 83 Farm Ridge Road in Westhampton? Might be connected to the homicide.

Jill: Random much?

Jill: Wait, are you at the old murder house?

I hit the call button as I walked back to the truck. Jill picked up on the first ring. "Murder house?" I demanded.

"Yeah, a serial killer lived out in Westhampton in the late eighties, early nineties," Jill replied. "He was a real nut job. Had a bait and tackle store on the main road, but underneath it was this tricked out bunker. He kept his kids and a few women captive there for years, thinking he was saving everyone from the end of the world."

"Really. How was he going to save it?"

"He claimed that some grand wizard came to him in his dreams and told him that all living men were evil, except him, of course."

"Of course."

"So he started picking off all the adult men he could find, and stashed the bodies in an old tobacco barn. He got away with it for a while, too, until one of his kids escaped the bunker and went to the cops. Hang on, I'll send you an article. There's a documentary, too."

"Thanks," I said, as I looked at the bright red tobacco barn next door. Never had I seen one painted in such an obnoxious shade. Maybe it was a warning. "Let me read it, and I'll call you back if I need to."

I got back in the truck as the article hit my inbox. It was an overview about how one Arthur Waterford went on a five -year murder spree before he was brought to justice. The writer did a follow-up piece with two of his kids a few years ago, the younger boy and a girl. No word on what the third kid was up to. The son in the interview was the one that escaped the bunker and put a stop to his father's killing. I scrolled to the last page, and saw the kids' names.

Arthur Junior and Francesca Waterford.

Waterford sounds a hell of a lot like Wexford.

Just in case that wasn't enough evidence, there were a couple recent pictures of the siblings. Arthur Waterford was one of our three victims.

"They must have changed their names," I muttered.

"What was that?" Dahlia asked.

I turned to Dahlia, and asked, "Did Francesca ever mention what went on here before there was a store?"

"Not really," she replied. "Just that it's an old family property that had bad memories."

I showed her the picture of Arthur Waterford. "Is this your boss's brother?"

"Yeah," she replied without hesitation. "He comes by the store sometimes. Someone wrote an article about him?"

"Turns out he was held captive by his father, who thought wizards told him to kill people," I said, as I forwarded the article to Eli.

"What?" Dahlia asked. "That's nuts!"

"Tell me about it," I began, then Jill called back. "Yeah?"

"The Arthur Wexford from your car accident," she began. "His body is gone."

"Gone? What do you mean, gone? Did someone take it?"

"Probably? The morgue was locked, and there's nothing on the security footage." She paused, and asked, "Why are you in Westhampton?"

"I am ninety-nine percent positive that the owner of the magic shop on Main Street is the serial killer's daughter," I replied. "She's been organizing witch hunts."

"Shit," Jill said. "Where's Eli?"

"Having tea with Bennet," I replied, as I started the engine. "They're at Tea on the Green. It's by—"

"I know where it is. I'll meet you there."

Jill ended the call as I pulled back onto the road and headed east. "If it's all right with you, I'm going straight to Eli," I said to Dahlia.

"It's fine," Dahlia said. "You need to make sure she's okay. I get it."

"If you see Francesca when we get there, or anyone else from that store, yell," I said. "Don't worry about them hurting you. I'm not going to let anything happen to you or anyone."

"What about Eli?" she asked. "Will she be safe with just Bennet to protect her?"

I laughed shortly. "If anything, Eli's the one protecting him."

Tea on the Green

T he best part about our afternoon plans was that since my car was sitting at home in the driveway, I got to drive Tessa's sports car to the teahouse.

"Have you ever driven something like this before?" Bennet asked, as we got into the car. It was a sleek grey model and so low to the ground I worried about getting it stuck in one of the town's many potholes. "This machine has a considerable amount of power."

"I can handle it," I said. "Tessa bought this car when we lived in Europe. We've done our fair share of traveling together."

"I see," Bennet said, then he withdrew his phone from his breast pocket and checked the screen. "Lillian said that she is already on her way to meet us."

"Good." I pulled out of the driveway, and navigated around a snowbank. "You two met at the bookstore café?"

"Yes, we did. There was very little seating in the café one day, and I ended up sharing a table with her and one of her friends. They asked me about the botany text I was reading, and we became friends."

"All three of you, or just you and Lillian?"

"Well, Lillian is the one I spend every Saturday afternoon with," he replied. "She and I have a great deal in common."

"Who would have thought, especially with your five-hundred-year age gap." I glanced at the shepherd in the passenger seat. "Have you mentioned anything about the supernatural to her yet?"

"No. I don't believe we've reached that level of familiarity as of yet. Although, she has been hinting that she would like to see my home. I don't know how I could explain the items in the front room, let alone the bedroom."

I coughed to hide my utter shock over Bennet inferring that Lillian would somehow see the interior of his bedroom. "Have you been to her place?"

"I have, but only to drop her off after our meetings. She has a lovely home."

"I bet." I squealed around a corner—Tessa's car was fun—and found a parking spot near the teahouse. "Sorry. That was dramatic."

"Eliza, you really should be more careful in your condition."

"Actually, thanks to the baby, I have a protection bubble. So far, it's kept me safe from exploding candles and a car accident."

"How wonderful. Will this bubble extend to me?"

"Point taken. I'll be more careful." We clambered out of the car—maybe it was *too* sleek and low, at least for a pregnant lady and an old shepherd—and headed toward the teahouse. "It seems like you really like Lillian."

"I do," he replied. "She's the first person I've felt I can be myself around in a very long time."

"You're not yourself around me?"

"Ah. I meant, in a more friendly capacity than what you and I share." Bennet held the door for me. Once we were inside, he approached the hostess. "Hello. We have a reservation under Carrington."

The hostess checked off something, then she grabbed some menus. There was a candle burning on the hostess stand, and it smelled like oranges. "Right this way," she said, and she led us to a table near the windows. "I'll send your server right over."

"Thank you," Bennet and I said in concert. I opened up the menu, and scanned the choices. "Is there something you usually order?" I asked.

"Lillian prefers the assortment with scones and petit fours," he began, then we heard the door chime. I looked toward the entrance, and saw Lillian herself.

I recognized her from her social media pictures. She had long brown hair with expensive-looking caramel highlights, and she was tall and slender. Her outfit was the sort of athleisure that rich mothers wore to pick up their kids from school, and her sneakers were pristine white. All in all, she was just as much an old money persona as her sister, the senator.

Lillian scanned the room, and grinned when she spotted Bennet. "Hey, Ben," she said, when she reached our table. "This your friend you wanted me to meet?"

"Yes, and hello to you, too." Bennet stood, and kissed her cheek before he pulled out her chair. "Lillian, this is Eliza Moore. Lyons! Her name is Eliza Lyons. I keep forgetting you're married now," he added.

"It's okay, Ben," I said, just to watch him blush. "It's nice to meet you, Lillian. Did Bennet tell you why I wanted to get together?"

"He said you're a detective, and working the murders that were found behind City Hall," she replied. "You don't think I had anything to do with that, do you?"

"I don't," I replied. "Also, full disclosure, I'm friends with Barbara. I'm the one that found Abby when she was kidnapped a few years ago."

"Ah." Lillian leaned back in her chair and sized me up as if I was a prized calf at the fair. "Are you one of Barbara's yes men?"

"Not in the least," I replied. "But the further we get into this case, the more it looks like your sister is being targeted. I was hoping that by us having a casual conversation, we might be able to figure out what's going on."

"Who's we?" she asked, as she twirled a length of caramel hair.

"My husband and I. We work and together." I handed her one of our cards.

Lillian took the card without reading it. "I really don't know how much help I'll be. Barbara and I really aren't close. We haven't been since she split with Abby's father."

"Really? Did they split because he was a jerk?"

"He really wasn't, but him and Barbara just weren't a good fit for each other. However," she continued, as she leaned closer, "the real issue between us was that I stayed friends with her former sister-in-law. We've always gotten along very well, and I think it made Barbara jealous."

"Family dynamics can be wacky," I said, then the server arrived and took our order. While I let Bennet navigate the intricacies of an English afternoon tea, I brought up pictures of the victims on my phone.

"Would you mind if I showed you pictures of the victims?" I asked Lillian, after the server departed. "One of them worked for your family."

Lillian paused. "They're not dead in the pictures, are they?"

"No, these are their license pictures."

"Oh, thank god. Yeah, sure, I'll have a look." I set my phone on the table, and showed her Jerry Goldman' picture. "He's our accountant," Lillian said right away. "My uncle thinks he's skimming money, but Jer covers his tracks pretty well." Lillian swallowed hard. "I-I guess he doesn't need to do that anymore."

Bennet patted her hand.

"I'm sorry," I said, then I swiped to Colleen's picture. "Do you recognize her?"

"No, but she looks familiar, if that makes any sense."

"It does. Her sister is Barbara's assistant, Megan."

"Weird," Lillian said. "Megan used to date Jer, but they had a blowout around a year ago."

"Really?" Yet another thing Megan deliberately hadn't told us. "Did Barbara know about their relationship?"

"Probably not. She only pays attention to herself." Lillian glanced at me. "Sorry. That sounded bratty."

"Don't worry about it. I am not here to judge your sibling relations." I swiped to Arthur Wexford's picture. "This is the third victim."

"No way! Artie died?" Lillian flopped back in her chair. "I had no idea!"

"Wait, you know him?"

"Yeah. He's my best friend's brother." Lillian turned to Bennet, and continued, "Remember my friend, Francesca? She was with me when we met at the bookstore. Artie was her little brother."

"This is Francesca Wexford, who runs a magic shop on Main Street?" I demanded.

"Yeah," Lillian said. "She's Barbara's former sister-in-law. Have you met her?"

Instead of replying, I sent Dan a text.

Eli: Get here now!

Dan: Already on my way. So is Jill.

Eli: Why Jill?

"Eliza?" Bennet asked. "What's wrong?"

"I'm not sure," I replied. "A bunch of clues just fell into place. I need to talk to Dan to get this straightened out." I rubbed my temple, wondering why my thoughts were so sluggish. "Jill's on her way, too."

"Jill Sanders, the police officer?" Bennet asked, then he rubbed the back of his neck. "My, it is warm in here."

"I feel like I should ask why the police are coming, but I can't figure out why that's a bad thing," Lillian said. "Do you think I'm dumb?"

"No. I think you're smart. Your hair's pretty, too," I added, then I pet Lillian's shiny brown hair. It was soft. Beyond her shoulder, I spied the burning candle, and recalled the candles I'd gotten at The Black Hat.

The spelled candles.

"Guys, I think we should go," I mumbled. "My protection bubble isn't bubbling."

"Huh?" Lillian asked, then the world went dark.

CAUSE OF DEATH: MANDRAGORINE

When Dahlia and I got to the teahouse, there were only two cars out front: Tessa's roadster, and a late model black Mercedes. I parked next to the Mercedes, and got out, then I noticed an acrid smell. I turned to the teahouse, and swore.

The front window was filled with smoke.

"Call nine one one," I yelled as I ran to the front door. It was locked, so I went back to my truck and popped the hatch, grabbed the crowbar and ran back to the door. I smashed a hole in the window to let the smoke out, then I beat on the lock until the door gave way. As soon as I was in, I pulled my shirt up over my nose and plunged into the smoke.

"Eli," I bellowed. No one answered, and the smoke was thick and visibility was close to nonexistent, but it wasn't hot. In fact, it reminded me of the smoke bombs my brothers and I used to set off behind the bakery when we were kids.

"Eli," I yelled. "Eliza! Bennet!"

No one spoke, but I heard something hit the floor. I followed the sound and found Eli, Bennet, and a woman I assumed was Lillian Stevens slumped over a table. A teapot lay shattered on the floor next to Bennet, which must have been what I heard. I picked up Eli and carried her toward the door.

"Is she okay?" Dahlia asked when I got outside.

"I think so." Eli was breathing, which was good. We would figure the rest out when the paramedics got here. I pulled down my shirt and breathed in some clean, cold air. "Two more are still inside. Open the truck's door for me?"

Dahlia opened the passenger side door, and as soon as I had Eli settled, I went back in. I'd just gotten to the front door when Jill arrived.

"Two more are inside," I yelled to Jill, then I went back into the teahouse. By the time I got to Bennet, Jill was next to me.

"This isn't smoke from a fire," Jill said. "This is more like the cold smoke you get from a fog machine."

"You take Lillian," I said; I would worry about what the smoke was made of after everyone was safe. I got Bennet over my shoulders in a fireman's carry and made my way toward the door. As soon as we were all outside, Dahlia opened the back door of Jill's car and I set Bennet inside.

"Help Jill," I yelled to Dahlia, then I went to Eli. She was pale, but her breathing was steady.

"Hey, baby," I said, as I patted her cheek. "Do me a favor and open your eyes. Please?"

Her eyes fluttered open, and I let myself exhale. "Dan?"

"I'm here. You're gonna be okay." I stroked her hair back from her face. "Do you know what happened?"

"I can feel him," she mumbled.

"Who? Bennet?"

"No." She took my hand and put it on her stomach. "Our baby. When the smoke got bad, I felt the bubble close in around him." She opened her eyes, and smiled. "He's okay. He's pretty smart, like you."

"Everyone knows you're the smart one," I said. "And the pretty one." I heard sirens; the fire department had arrived.

"There's a candle on the hostess stand," Eli said. "It's citrus like the shop candles. I think it's the catalyst for all this smoke."

"I'll make sure Jill grabs it for us." I kissed Eli's forehead. "I love you, baby. Stay here and rest."

"Okay," she said, then her eyes closed. I squeezed her hand, and went in search of Jill. I found her standing next to the fire chief.

"This is not how I thought my day would go," Jill said.

"Me, neither," I said, then I murmured, "There's a candle on the hostess station. We, ah, need it."

"I'll see what I can do," Jill said. "How's Eli?"

"She's coming out of it. How are the other two?"

"Perking up now that they're in the fresh air. And why is Lillian Stevens here?"

"Believe it or not, her and Bennet are dating."

"Interesting." Jill pulled out her phone. "I have to call this in."

"Yell if you need me," I said, then I went to check on Lillian and Bennet. They were a bit dazed, but seemed otherwise unharmed, and they had the added benefit of Dahlia standing over them like a mother hen. Since those three were all set for the time being, I went back to my wife. Her big brown eyes were wide open as she watched the smoke billowing out of the place's front door and into the sky.

"Hey, you're all the way awake," I said, as I crouched down next to her. "Do you remember what happened in there?"

"Oh, yeah. First of all, Lillian is not the airhead Barbara thinks she is. I think her and Bennet really like each other."

"Opposites attract, I guess."

"They sure do. Most importantly, though, Lillian told me that Arthur Wexford is her friend Francesca Wexford's brother! Also, Francesca is Barbara's former sister-in-law."

"Holy shit," I said.

"Wait, there's more. Megan Bergquist used to date Jerry the accountant slash victim number three."

"Why does Megan keep hiding things?" I wondered out loud. "All these little details would have helped us out in the beginning."

"Tell me about it. You don't think she's the killer, do you?"

"I don't get a killer vibe from Megan," I replied. "More of a kid who's afraid of getting caught." I took Eli's hand. "You can really feel the baby?"

"Yeah," she said, as she smiled. "First time, too. But he's in there, and he's not going anywhere. He's stubborn like you."

"That's right, he is." The fact that my wife and my kid were safe made me simultaneously relieved, and terrified that something else might happen to them. "So guess what we learned out in Westhampton?"

"I can only imagine."

"These Wexford siblings are the spawn of a local serial killer. He built a doomsday bunker beneath a bait and tackle shop, and kept his kids imprisoned there. Told everyone wizards made him kill a few guys and kidnap their girlfriends."

"What the... Dan, this case is insane."

"Yes it is, and that's why I think we should walk away from it."

"What?" Eli shook her head. "No, Dan, we have to solve it!"

"Do we?" I asked. "You've already been hit by a car, picked up exploding candles and poisoned water, and now this. Would this smoke have killed you? Or was it just to knock you out so someone could abduct you?" I leaned closer, and asked, "Is this smoke how they subdued our three victims before they strung them up?"

Eli bit her bottom lip. "I don't know the answers to any of that. But I don't feel right letting this Francesca asshole walk free."

"She won't. We'll tell Jill everything we know, then we'll let the cops handle it." I reached over and caressed Eli's cheek. "I waited my entire life for you. I don't want to lose you."

"I don't want to lose you, either." Eli set her hand on mine. "We should have Tessa check out this latest spelled candle, though. She could probably track the ingredients, or something."

"Or something." I glanced toward the first responders, and saw Jill walking toward us. She stopped next to us, and handed Eli a plastic evidence bag.

"Here's the candle," Jill said. "You didn't get it from me. How are you feeling?"

"Woozy," Eli replied. "I don't like woozy."

"Woozy is better than dead," Jill said. "And I bring other news."

"Good news?" I asked hopefully.

"Depends. Cause of death came in for the three hanging victims, and it was poison. Specifically, they all had an abundance of the alkaloids scopolamine and mandragorine in their systems. Also, you were right, Dan. The coroner determined that they were all dead for at least a day before they were strung up."

Sometimes, I really hated being right. "We were just discussing dropping this case. Too many close calls, you know?"

"I get it," Jill began, but Eli shook her head.

"We need to keep investigating," Eli said. "If they all had mandragorine in their system, that means mandrake contributed to their deaths. That moves this case back into my territory." She looked at me, and continued, "As Mistress of Seers, I need to see this through. It's my duty to hold accountable anyone who misuses baneful herbs."

I blew out a breath and rubbed the back of my neck. I understood her point of view, and her responsibilities to the supernatural community, but I didn't like it. "All right. We're staying on, but we're going to go about this in the most careful way possible."

Eli grinned. "You're the best."

"Only for you," I replied. "What we all need to do it sit down, share all of our information, and make a plan so we can solve this case and keep anyone else—namely you—from getting hurt. Let's get this scene wrapped up, then we'll worry about the next steps."

"Sounds good," Jill said. "Let me get an update from the fire chief, and I'll see about getting everyone out of here. Hang tight, guys."

After Jill was out of earshot, I turned to Eli. "You can't let it go, not even for the baby?"

"I'm doing this for the baby," she said. "If we don't stop this now, our kid could be the next victim."

I wiped my hand down my face. Yeah, we were bringing a supernatural child into the world, as if having a kid wasn't already stressful and scary enough. "We can't fight off every bigot in the world," I said. "Even if we could, there's better ways to spend our lives."

"I know," she said. "But this is a bigot who's close to home, and it's looking like she's already killed. If we can stop her now, we'll make the entire world a better place for everyone, including our baby."

"All right," I said, not that it was ever hard for Eli to sway me to her side. I kissed the back of her hand. "Let's get out of here, and find a quiet place where we can take a step back and talk."

Eli leaned over and kissed me. "Thank you, for believing in me."

"Always, baby." I said. Inside, I hoped we weren't playing into the killer's hands.

Thirst

After the fire department got the situation at the tea house under control, Jill, Lillian, Bennet, Dahlia, Dan, and I all went to my and Dan's house. Soon we would know if our driveway really could fit four cars, because few of us were smart enough to carpool.

Actually, it would need to fit five vehicles, since my car was already there. The neighbors were going to think we were having a party. I hoped no one felt left out.

The main difference on this journey as opposed to the one to the teahouse was that Bennet rode with Lillian, and Dahlia hitched a ride with me in Tessa's fancy sports car. Poor Dan was stuck driving alone, but I think he preferred it that way. He turns his music up way too loud, anyway. Jill was also driving solo, but she was in a police cruiser. I'm sure having guests in those vehicles was not encouraged.

"This is a really nice car," Dahlia said, as she ran her hands over the dashboard. "Do all witches get cars like this?"

"It's not a witch thing, so much as it's a money thing," I replied. "Tessa is loaded, and it has nothing to do with witchcraft. Back in the day, she was a countess."

"Oh, you mean before she was a witch?"

"You're born a witch. You don't become one." I glanced at Dahlia. "If you have questions about witchy stuff, fire away. I don't mind curiosity."

"You don't think it's rude?"

"Not if you ask nicely."

"Okay." Dahla paused for a moment. "Spells. How do you learn them? Is there a witch school, where you learn how to cast them? And do you have to memorize whole books of them?"

"No, to the last two, but a magic school would be super fun. As for how we learn spells, magic isn't really about spells. It's about energy, and learning how to manipulate it. The best way it's ever been described to me is that magic works off of intent and emotion," I added, paraphrasing something Jacob Allwood once told me. "The stronger you feel about what you're doing, the stronger your spells will be."

"Where does the energy for spells come from?"

"It's all around us. Have you ever taken science classes where they talk about matter and energy, and how nothing can really be created or destroyed?" Dahlia murmured that she had. "It's like that."

"Huh. Does that mean that people like me can use this energy, too?"

"If you're asking if you can learn how to wield magic, the answer is yes," I replied. "It's a skill that can be harnessed by anyone, though witches do have a leg up on mortals, since we're so much more sensitive to natural energies."

"I never thought about it that way," she murmured. "What happened with those stinking candles you brought back to the store? Did you put a spell on them?"

"Quite the opposite. When I used magic to light them, they exploded."

"Oh, my god! Are you okay?"

"Yeah. I stopped the explosions. And here we are." I pulled into the driveway right behind Dan's truck. Jill and Lillian arrived a moment later. "Fair warning, we have a dog, and he will be your best friend."

"Cool," Dahlia said. "I like dogs."

We all got out of our respective vehicles, then I sent Tessa a text letting her know where her car was, and that we had yet another spelled candle to deal with. Dan led everyone toward the kitchen door. As soon as he opened it, Stuart barreled outside to greet everyone.

"Oh, what a cute puppy," Dahlia said, as she knelt down to pet him. Seeing that he'd already won her over, Stuart commenced licking her. "He's so excited!"

"This is Stuart," Dan said, as he picked him up and carried him inside. "He doesn't bite, but he may lick you to death. Everyone, have a seat. The living room is just through that door."

The other four arranged themselves on the couch while Dan fed Stuart a few treats and I drank a glass of water.

"How do you feel?" Dan asked.

"Fine, which is kind of weird," I replied. "I assumed there would be some kind of aftereffect from the smoke, but I'm just really thirsty."

"If you feel off in any way, you let me know," Dan said, as he draped his arms across my shoulders. "Remember, I'm in charge here."

"Oh, are you?"

"Yes, because I'm older. Seniority, and all."

I stood on my toes and kissed him. "All right, old guy. Let's see if your geriatric brain can figure out what's happening here."

After we played the good hosts and got everyone something to drink, we sat with the rest in a loose circle. It reminded me of the gathering Francesca organized in The Black Hat's basement, except that we weren't evil bigots.

"Lillian," I began. "You told me that Francesca Wexford is Barbara's former sister-in-law. Does that mean Barbara was married to Artie?"

"Wait," Jill said. "This Artie is Arthur Wexford? The senator is related to one of the hanging victims?"

"We're not really related, not anymore," Lillian said. "Barbara and Jared split up a while ago. But yeah, Francesca is Artie's older sister. Artie was the baby of the family."

Jill leaned back and rubbed her eyes. "This is going to be a media circus."

"Maybe not," Lillian said. "When Jared went into medical school, he changed his name. There was some drama with his family a few years ago, and he didn't want stuff that happened when he was a kid to overshadow his career."

"Smart move," I said. "Speaking of people who are tangentially related to Barbara, remember Megan Bergquist? She dated one of the other victims, who also happens to be the Stevens's accountant."

"That's it, I'm calling Megan in," Jill said, as she whipped out a notebook and started writing furiously. "She's withheld too many facts, and it's pissing me off."

"I totally agree." I went to the kitchen and refilled my glass. While I was in there, I heard Dan ask Lillian to describe what she saw when she arrived at the teahouse.

"When I first got there, everything was business as usual," Lillian began. "The regular Saturday hostess was at the door." She glanced at Jill. "Did everyone get out in time?"

"No one was there but you three," Jill replied. "No employees in the front, no one in the kitchen or storeroom, and no cars were parked out back. We're working to track down everyone who was supposed to be working, and get their statements."

"Do you think someone warned them?" I asked, between sips of water.

"Maybe," Jill replied. "Lillian, did you notice anything out of the ordinary?"

"Oh, yeah. The candle at the hostess station was smoking. I thought it was weird, but the employees were all ignoring it, so I thought it was okay."

"And the candle proceeded to emit a vapor that incapacitated all of us," Bennet said. "Eli, you said the candles you purchased at The Black Hat exploded when you lit them. When we entered the teahouse, the candle wasn't smoking, yet some time after you passed it, it became noxious. It would appear that you were the catalyst for the smoke."

"I get what you're saying, but how could I be the catalyst?" I drained my glass, and went back for a refill. "How would anyone set that up?" I returned to the living room's doorway, and instead of anyone offering their insights, they were all staring at me. "What?"

"Eliza," Dan said. "You just drank about forty ounces of water in less than five minutes."

"Oh." I looked at the glass in my hand. "That's a lot, huh?"

"I'm calling Angel," Jill said. "Maybe the fumes dehydrated you."

"If she's that dehydrated, she should go to a hospital," Dan said.

"If this is magical dehydration, we're all better off staying off the record," Jill said, as she put her phone to her ear. Angel picked up, and Jill went into the other room to talk to her.

I turned to Dan, who was frowning up a storm. "If Angel says I need a hospital, I'll go," I said. "No arguments. But Jill has a point. Besides, the last time I went to a hospital, that creepy Dr. Besami took a vial of my blood."

"Dr. Besami?" Lillian repeated. "Jared Besami? Average height, dark hair, kinda geeky?"

"Yeah. Why?"

"That's Barbara's ex-husband."

I stared at Lillian, because I just figured out exactly how the candle was spelled to smoke after I passed by it. I faced Bennet, and asked, "If my blood was added to a candle designed to knock us out—"

"There's no telling what other spells were created," Bennet finished. "How much blood is in a vial?"

"I have no flipping idea." My thoughts were whirling inside my brain, making me dizzy. I set down my glass and grasped my head, trying to slow everything down so I could think. "This is really bad."

"All right," Dan said. "What do we do?"

"We need to locate this Dr. Besami, and reclaim Eli's blood," Bennet replied.

A Drain Spell?

By the time Angel arrived at the house, complete with bags of saline solution and one of those IV stands straight from the hospital, I was so dried out my skin was flaking.

"Eliza, exactly how did you get yourself into such a state?" Angel asked, as she got the IV set up. "You're far too healthy to get this dehydrated this fast."

"Would you believe magical smoke?" I asked. I was sitting in the recliner in the living room, next to the front window. Dan had relocated everyone else into the kitchen so Angel would have room to work. "Also, I've had like sixty ounces of water in the past hour and haven't gone to the bathroom once. That's weird, right?"

"Very." Angel picked up my wrist and felt my pulse, then she got out a blood pressure cuff.

"Are you worried I have high blood pressure?"

"Low, actually. Dehydration does that." While she inflated the cuff, she called over her shoulder, "Dan, bring us some ice chips, please. And if you have any Gatorade or other sports drinks, that would be good, too."

"Thanks for coming over," I said, while Angel checked the reading. "I know this is your day off. I really appreciate it."

"It is my pleasure," Angel said, as she deflated the cuff. "Any friend of Jill's is a friend of mine, and you do keep that man of yours in line."

"I don't know about that," I said. "Dan's a loose cannon."

Angel smiled at me, then she checked the saline bag. It was nearly empty. "Where is all this fluid going?" she murmured.

"Does she need to go to the hospital?" Dan demanded, as he strode into the room with a bowl of ice chips.

"I'm honestly not sure," Angel replied. "I don't understand how Eli is ingesting copious amounts of fluid, yet it is having no effect on you. It's like you're a bucket with a hole in the bottom."

"Well, this reinforces that it's a magical cause, not mundane," I said. I rubbed my forearm, and skin peeled away as if I had a three-day-old sunburn. "What's also strange is that I don't feel sick, just thirsty."

Angel raised an eyebrow. "Dan, feed her some ice. While you do that, tell me any other recent symptoms she's had, no matter how odd or unrelated you think they are."

"She's pregnant, for one," Dan said.

"And there's something you could have brought up earlier," Angel said, with a disapproving glance at me. "Have you had any complications?"

"I don't think so," I replied. "I had an ultrasound, and they said everything looked good. Although, it was the evil doctor that told me that."

"The doctor was evil? What makes you say that?"

"Apparently, he's related to the woman who's organizing witch hunts in town," I replied. "We also think he has a vial of my blood and is using it to create spells that specifically target me."

"What is this doctor's name?" Angel asked.

"Jared Besami."

Angel stared at me for a moment, then she whipped out her phone and walked out to the porch to make a call.

"I think I blew her mind," I said to Dan.

"I don't know if that's possible," Dan said. "Angel's one of the toughest people I know. She has to be, to put up with Jill."

"I heard that," Jill yelled from the kitchen.

"Good, because I meant it," Dan yelled back. "In other news, Lillian seems quite unbothered by all of this talk about magic."

"Yeah, I noticed that," I said. "Maybe Bennet talked to her on the way over."

"Maybe." He fed me another ice chip, then he stroked my hair. "Even your hair is dry. What's the purpose behind this?"

"There might not be a real purpose," I said. "It could be an unintended side effect, which happens a lot when inexperienced people try to cast spells. Or its whole purpose could be to annoy and distract, in which case this spell's a banger."

Dan leaned in and kissed my forehead. "You sure you feel okay? How's the protection bubble?"

I patted my belly. "Still there."

"I just spoke with the front desk at the hospital," Angel said, as she reentered the room. "Besami hasn't worked a shift in more two months. And you said he gave you an ultrasound?"

"I saw him in the emergency room, after the car accident," I began.

"You were in a car accident?" Angel demanded. "Eliza, I don't know what you've gotten into lately, but you need to be careful in your condition. I'm putting you on bedrest."

"Hey!"

"Thank you," Dan said, over me. "Tell her we need to stop investigating this case, too."

"Now that would be a bad idea," Angel said. "If you're lying around all day with nothing to do, it can drive you absolutely batty. That would only add more stress to Eliza and the baby. Therefore, I believe you should keep investigating, but Eliza needs work from home."

"That still sounds boring," I said.

"I know, but boring and alive is much better than exciting and dead," Angel said. "How far along are you?"

"Thirteen weeks."

"Second trimester, then." Angel sat on the arm of the chair. "You two think about names yet?"

"Not really," I replied. "Dan Junior, maybe?"

Dan laughed shortly. "I figured you'd want Alexander."

"What if it turns out to be a girl?" Angel asked.

"It's a boy," I said. "Witch's intuition."

"Well, let's hope your intuition keeps you out of any further calamities," she said. "Oh, my friend in hematology is going to try and locate your blood sample. Would you prefer her to destroy it, or bring it here to you?"

"I think destroying is the better option," I replied. "Angel, you really are the best."

"I know, and don't you forget it."

Our visitors left shortly afterward. I was sure Angel was tired from her string of late-night shifts at the hospital, and Bennet and Lillian had plenty to talk about. Jill was headed back to the station, but she agreed to drop Dahlia off at home. Then, it was just me and Mr. Over Protective.

"Want me to carry you upstairs?" he asked, after he refilled my bowl of ice chips. "And have you peed yet?"

"No, and no," I replied. I was perfectly capable of walking, and I'd just tried to go to the bathroom. Nothing. I felt sparks at the base of my skull, and grabbed my phone. "I'm calling Jacob. My foresight thinks it's a good idea."

"Your foresight is the only thing that makes sense around here, and that is terrifying," Dan muttered.

"Tell me about it," I said, as I hit the call button.

"Good afternoon, Eli," Jacob said by way of greeting. "How are you doing?"

"So I've got a situation here, and it might be a magical problem," I said. "Have you ever heard about someone drinking gallons of water, and it having no effect on them?"

Jacob's spirit appeared in front of me. This disappearing water must be a bigger deal than I'd realized. "How long has this been going on?"

"About an hour," I replied. "I'm as dry as a desert, and I've had literal gallons of water, ice chips, this gross electrolyte drink—"

"A nurse described Eli as a bucket with a hole in the bottom," Dan interjected.

Jacob nodded. "You do look like a scarecrow with that dry hair."

"Thanks," I said. "This must be some sort of spell, right?"

"It sounds like someone is attempting to drain your power, but the spell has latched onto moisture rather than magic," Jacob mused. "It's not an uncommon or particularly difficult spell, but it does require a portion of the subject's body—hair, or nail clippings, for instance—in order to work."

"Um." I glanced at Dan. His face told me he was furious. "The hospital has a vial of my blood."

"What?" Jacob demanded. He reached for his phone, but he must have left it behind at home. "Call LeClerc and tell him everything. Now. We need to get your blood back immediately."

"On it," Dan said, as he walked into the kitchen to make the call. Jacob approached me, and held my head as he scrutinized my face.

"What are you doing?" I asked.

"Looking for further signs of decline," he replied, as he released me. "Eliza, this is very serious. You have Allwood blood in your veins. If some dark actor has possession of your blood, they could potentially harm everyone you're blood related to."

"My dad," I said, then I called him. He didn't pick up, so I left him a rambling voice message. As soon as that was done, I called Tess.

"Yes?" she greeted.

"An evil doctor has my blood and Dad is in danger," I said. "They took my blood while I was in the emergency department, and now there's a spell on me that's draining." I looked beseechingly at Jacob. "A drain spell?"

"The spell is most likely supposed to drain her magical aptitude, but it's draining all of the moisture from her body instead," Jacob said loudly enough for Tessa to hear. "It appears to be progressing rapidly."

"Merde," Tessa muttered. "We'll right there."

"No," I said. "I need you to protect Dad!"

"Eli, Alex can handle himself."

"I know he can, but he is the sole living marksman," I said, referencing my father's position in the seer hierarchy. The only person more powerful than him was me, as Mistress of Seers. "This spell isn't meant for him, and it might skip him entirely, but if something happens to me, the seers will need Dad to lead them."

"Eli," Tess and Jacob said at the same time.

"Promise me, Tess," I said.

"I'll explain the situation to Alex now. Talk soon." With that, Tess disconnected. I looked at Jacob, and fought the urge to burst into tears.

"We are going to beat this," Jacob said, as he embraced me. "We will reclaim your blood, and end this enchantment."

"What's happening?" Dan demanded. I looked up from where my face had been pressed into Jacob's shoulder, and saw Dan standing in the kitchen doorway with his phone in his hand.

"The spell is draining me, just like Angel thought," I said, as I wiped my cheek against my shoulder. My skin was so dry and fragile, my soft tee shirt felt like sandpaper being dragged across my cheek. "Since they have my blood, they can go after everyone I'm related to."

"Shit," Dan said, as he pulled me into his arms. "I never should have let the paramedics take you. This is all my fault."

"It's not," I said, as I pressed my face against his chest. "You were only trying to help me. It's not your fault Besami stole my blood."

"Besami?" Jacob said. "That's the one who did this?"

"We think it was either him, or Francesca Wexford," I replied. "They're siblings."

"I told LeClerc about the doctor," Dan said. "What can we do for Eli now?"

"We must protect her," Jacob said. "Encase her in a bubble, so to speak."

"I already have a protection bubble," I said. "Right now, it's close to my baby, but before this drain spell happened, it surrounded my entire body."

Jacob's brows peaked, then he glanced at my midsection, and nodded. "Then we must convince the baby to make the bubble once again big enough for two."

Back to the Lab

Yet again, we were dividing and conquering. It was my least favorite way to solve a problem, but until we put a lid on whatever was happening with Eli, she needed to stay home while Jacob and I did the grunt work. Man, she was pissed about that.

"Is LeClerc meeting us at the hospital?" I asked Jacob. He and I were en route to the hospital in an attempt gain access to the lab, and find the vial of Eli's blood the emergency room doctors had drawn.

"He's not," Jacob replied. "I've tasked him with finding Besami's home address, and having a look around the property. Since LeClerc can change locations instantly, he is a better choice for reconnaissance work than you are, at the moment. And Besami won't be able to hurt him."

"He's also probably not expecting a ghost to break into his house, either."

"Probably not. How did you make the connection between this Dr. Besami being the brother of the owner of the magic shop?"

"That was all due to something you said," I replied. "I went out to West-hampton to check out the magic shop's former location, mostly because you said there used to be some anti-witch group out there. Turns out Besami's father was a serial killer who thought a wizard was telling him to murder people."

"Ah, yes. The Waterford killings. As I recall, not a single one of his victims was a witch, and this supposed wizard only existed in Waterford's mind." Jacob sighed. "While it was good for our community to be wholly exonerated, Waterford's actions were devastating to the mortal town. It took years for the area to recover."

"I can imagine." My phone beeped. I glanced at the screen, and saw a text from Jill asking me to call. I did, and she picked up immediately.

"Is Angel with you?" Jill demanded.

"No. I thought she left when you did?"

"She did, but she's not home yet. Even if she stopped someplace, she should be back by now."

"You call her?"

"About a thousand times. All went straight to voice mail." Jill paused. "Dan, I'm worried."

"Me, too," I said. Angel was nothing if not reliable. It wasn't like her to take off without telling anyone where she was headed, or to not pick up Jill's calls. "I'm headed to the hospital now. Think she stopped by there?"

"Maybe. Why are you going there? Is Eli okay?"

"Eli is home trying to relax." I pictured Eli sitting on our bed, trying to meditate, while Stuart whined for attention. "I'm going to steal back her blood."

"I'm not bailing you out when you get caught."

"Bullshit. You will and you know it."

"Fine. Call me if you hear from my missing wife."

Jill hung up. I glanced at Jacob, and said, "Odd that Angel's gone radio silent."

"Do you think it's related to Eli's situation?"

"Maybe. Probably. What the hell do I know. I'm just the clueless mortal." I blew out a breath. "Sorry. I don't mean to vent at you. It's just been a tough day."

"Please, vent all you'd like," Jacob said. "You're just as much of an Allwood now as Eli. We're family, and family is always there for one another."

If anyone had told me a year ago that hearing such a declaration from a witch who was also ghost would have warmed my heart, I would have told them to quit drinking. Now, I just smiled. "Thanks, Jacob. That means a lot."

"Think nothing of it." Jacob drummed his fingers on his thigh. "Have you learned anything additional about this individual calling himself Jared Besami?"

"Did your foresight tell you to ask me that?"

"Actually, yes. It did. It seems that your own intuition has also been refined of late."

"More like I'm on high alert for signs of the next debacle. Anyway, Besami is the ex-husband of Senator Stevens."

Jacob paused. "Didn't Eli rescue the senator's child a few years ago?"

"Yeah. You heard about that?"

"I remember the supernatural community being up in arms over Eli's actions," Jacob replied. "Helena had already passed on, but Alexander was still traveling the world as the marksman, and Eli made no attempt to take on the role of Mistress of Seers. Some argued that Eli had abandoned her calling altogether, while others claimed her mortal mother had too strong of an influence on her."

"What was your opinion?"

"Ah. At the time, I'd yet to meet Eli, but I had known Helena quite well. I was confident that Eli would do what was right, and that the rest of the community needed to be patient." Jacob blew out a breath, an odd move for a ghost. "I do regret not reaching out to Eli during that time. We didn't yet know we were related, but as the head of my clan, I should have attempted to make some inroads with her."

"Don't beat yourself up. I'm sure you had plenty going on in your own family that kept you busy." I pulled into the hospital's parking lot, and went toward the employee parking area. "Eli's foresight told her that the senator's a victim in all of this."

"I suppose that makes sense, what with her ex-husband being involved."

"It's more than just him. Out of our three homicide victims, one was her former brother-in-law, one was her accountant, and the third was her assistant's sister. Oh, and don't forget," I added. "Besami's real name is Waterford. He's the eldest child of the Westhampton serial killer."

Jacob grunted. "That is quite interesting, especially the part about Besami's father. But I wonder, has the senator offended anyone in the supernatural community?"

"Not that I know of. Why? What happens when you offend a witch?"

"It would depend on the witch in question, but it appears that someone is going to great lengths to destroy the senator's legacy."

I parked, cut the engine, and faced Jacob. "You know, her sister is running for mayor. The two of them don't get along. She—the sister, that is—is also dating Bennet Carrington."

Jacob frowned. "That is quite concerning. Let's work quickly here, and then drop in on our shepherd."

The two of us entered the hospital, and walked toward the hematology department. "Have you ever been inside a blood lab?" I asked.

"No, I don't believe I have," Jacob replied. "I assume you want me to gain entry, and search for the blood vial?"

"Might be easier if you take point on this."

"Agreed. Wait here."

I took a seat in the waiting room as Jacob faded from view. Frankly, I had no idea what the inside of the lab looked like. Hopefully, the samples were organized alphabetically, and Jacob would be able to find Eli's vial without too much trouble. While I sat there trying to look casual, none other than Jared Besami himself entered the waiting room.

"Hey, Dr. Besami," I called, because I was a born troublemaker. The good doctor stopped in his tracks when he saw me walking toward him. "How are you doing today?"

"I'm well," he replied, a bit warily. "Mr. Lyons, is that right?"

"You got it," I said, grinning the entire time. "Listen, I wanted to thank you for how well you took care of my wife the other day. Man, I was so worried about her and the baby, but you fixed her right up."

"Of course. That's our job, after all." He glanced around the waiting room. "Is your wife here?"

"No, she's at work." I watched Besami's brow pinch; I'd confused him. Good. "I gave a family member a lift here."

"I see," Besami said. "Well, it was good seeing you, Mr. Lyons. I'm glad your wife is doing well. Please tell her I said hello."

"You got it," I said, and I watched Besami enter the lab. That interaction left me with two questions. One, if Besami hadn't picked up any shifts in two months, why did I run into him at the hospital twice in less than a week? And two, why was he confused about Eli being at work?

Suddenly, Jacob was sitting beside me. "Were you just trying to jump scare me?" I asked.

"Now Dan, would I really do that?" he asked, in return. "I have unsettling news. I've surveyed the entire inventory, and Eli's sample is not present."

"You were gone less than five minutes. How did you check everything so fast?" Jacob gave me a look. Right. Magic. "Here's some more unsettling news. Besami is here."

Jacob scanned the waiting room. "Where?"

"He went through that door," I said, then, as if on cue, Besami walked out the door and left the waiting room. "That's him."

"Wait here," Jacob said. He followed Besami, on foot this time. While he was gone, I texted Eli a pink heart. She texted back a blue one. While I was grinning at my phone, Jacob returned.

"That individual is not Besami," Jacob said. "I don't know who they are, but they're wearing a glamour. I suppose it could be Besami wearing a glamour of himself, but I can't fathom why one would do so."

"And since that person recognized me, Fake Besami was probably who we saw in the emergency department," I concluded. "How can we find out who's underneath the magic?"

"The glamour was too strong for me to penetrate," Jacob replied. "Whoever cast it is either very strong, or the wearer has a charm on their person keeping the image intact."

"We'll have to follow him," I said as I stood, but Jacob shook his head.

"I managed to put a magical tracker on him. We can follow him that way, safely and from a distance."

"Not bad. I'll make a detective out of you yet."

Jacob laughed. "I've solved my share of mysteries over the decades. Should we check in on the shepherd now?"

"That is a great plan."

QUENCHED

As soon as Dan and Jacob were out the door, I went into the guest room and sat in the center of the bed, intending to meditate on my current situation and hopefully find a way out of it. I'd been in my fair share of predicaments, but this magical dehydration was unreal. Sensing that something was wrong, Stuart hopped up beside me to lend moral support.

"Hey, buddy," I said, as I rubbed his ears. "You liked having new people over, didn't you?" He whuffed, and set his paw on my knee. "I have to be quiet for a bit, but you can stay with me. No barking, okay?"

Stuart laid down so his head was on my thigh. I closed my eyes, and visualized the inside of my body. The pictures that played in my mind's eye weren't anatomically correct, but I wasn't interested in my veins and organs. I was interested in what was happening to me magically. As soon as my trance was deep enough, I dove into the magical miasma that was drying me out.

First, I checked on my baby. He was sleeping like an angel, curled up in a white blanket and surrounded by the protection bubble. I gave the bubble a poke; it shimmered, but remained intact. Reassured that he was safe, I moved on to my digestive system.

Since I was near my baby, I figured I was somewhere in my abdomen. I looked up toward my throat, which resembled a high tower with an oculus set in the roof. That hole must represent my mouth. I swept my gaze downward, and saw another hole at the base. Huh. So the magical equivalent of my throat and stomach currently resembled a storm drain, and it was whisking water out of my system as quickly as I drank it.

But where had this drain come from? And more importantly, where does it end up?

Intrigued, I moved lower in my magical self. The bottom part of my gastrointestinal tract resembled a construction zone with bricks and debris scattered in front of a retaining wall. That wall had a huge opening in the center that was not supposed to be there. Someone had magically blown a hole in my system.

"Rude," I muttered. I picked up a brick and set it in place on the remains of the wall. I replaced a few more bricks while smiling to myself because hey, wasn't this an easy fix, when the bricks crumbled apart and fell into the hole. I, or rather my foresight, realized that whoever had blown this hole in my system was also the person draining my moisture, drop by drop. Logically, their magical signature would be at the bottom of the hole, so I climbed onto the wall, and jumped.

Free falling is an amazing rush, especially when it's not your physical body hurtling toward the ground at high velocity. I'd always wanted to try skydiving, but every so often a news article popped up about a skydiver whose parachute didn't open in time, and splat! What an awful way to go.

Speaking of going, I'd been falling for an awfully long time. Where could this hole possibly end up? I held my arms out to either side, and willed myself to slow down. Soon enough, I was hovering in midair, and there was an entrance to a tunnel across from me. It was the only offshoot from the main line I'd come across, so I propelled myself into it.

I emerged from the darkness of the tunnel into the most well lit room in the history of rooms. There were no windows, but the walls and ceiling were bright white, and the overhead fluorescent light made the place nearly blinding. A pipe labelled "water" ran across the ceiling, and it had sprung a leak at the far end. Oddly enough, the floor was soft brown dirt, like what you'd find in an already tilled field. It was quite muddy underneath the leak, but the rest of the room was dry. In the corner, three kids were huddled together.

The kids were two boys and a girl. The youngest boy looked to be about three years old, while the eldest boy was about ten years old. However, the girl—the apparent middle child—was the one in charge. Or at least, she thought she was.

"This is going to work," the girl said, as she comforted the youngest. He was bawling in her arms. "If we cause a big enough leak in the pipes, the water company will come out to fix it, and they'll find us."

"What if they don't come out?" the older boy asked. "What if no one's working today, or what if we drown before they get here? We need a backup plan."

"Fine," the girl snapped. "What do you want to do?"

"I'll shimmy out of the crawlspace and go for help," he said. "We're right next to the main road. A police station or a store has got to be close by."

I took another look around the room, and realized that these three children were the Waterford kids plotting their escape from where they'd been imprisoned by their father. According to the story, their deranged father had stashed them in an underground bunker, and the oldest child had busted out and gotten help.

That oldest child was Jared Besami, and his siblings were Arthur and Francesca Wexford.

I approached the kids, and said, "Looks like you've gotten yourselves into quite a pickle."

The boys screamed, but Francesca remained cool as a cucumber. "I wasn't expecting to see you here."

"Likewise." My gaze skated around the room. The water flowed faster, and the place was rapidly becoming a swimming pool. "Let me guess, you were trying to siphon off my magic, but since this water-based caper is a core memory of yours, you're draining all the moisture from my body, instead?"

"It's not my fault the spell went wrong," she snapped. "I was born good, and not a filthy witch like you!"

Didn't that admission clear up a bunch of questions. "Why did you kill the three people you left behind City Hall, and make them look like witches?"

"They may as well have been witches." Francesca railed at me. "They were always looking for shortcuts! Buying spells, trying to predict the future! It was disgusting."

"One of those victims was your brother," I said. "How is you murdering your sibling not disgusting?"

"Artie fell in with a witch," she snapped. "Kept saying he loved her, that he would marry her as soon as she was released from prison. After everything that happened to us because of witches, he still took up with one! I couldn't let that go unpunished."

"You didn't punish him. You killed him!"

"He's in a better place now." Francesca stood, and her appearance morphed from a little girl into that of Cecily Allwood. "And now I wear his lover's face."

"That is seriously messed up," I began, then I realized that this witch hating mortal could manage some seriously good glamours. "That's a very good impersonation of Cecily. Can you do anyone else?"

"I can take on the appearance of anyone I have a piece of," she replied.

"Piece?" I asked. "As in, something they touched?"

"Of course not. I need part of their body." Francesca bared her teeth. "Hair, bone... blood. It all works."

"Cool," I said, as I inwardly screamed. "Can you do me?"

"I will be able to, soon enough."

That response told me that Francesca already had my blood, but she needed to do something with it before she could impersonate me. That meant I had time to stop her.

"Okay, well, good luck with that." I turned away from her and examined the water pipe. It was already leaking, but there was an overflow valve at the far end, and I wanted to open it all the way.

"What are you doing?" Francesca asked.

"Since this core memory of yours is also what's draining me, I'm thinking that if I bust the water main wide open, it will kick you out of this loop, and end your lame ass spell at the same time," I replied. At least, I hoped that's what was going to happen. I approached the water main and grabbed the valve, and pulled the wheel to the right. Francesca shrieked as gallons of water poured into the basement bunker, but I stood motionless in front of the spray. Finally, I was quenched.

I woke from my trance as if I'd surfaced after swimming underwater, exhausted and gasping for breath. And I was soaked. My hair, my clothes, the bed, and poor Stuart were all positively waterlogged, as if we'd physically been in that flooded bunker.

"Sorry, Stuart," I said, as the bewildered dog wondered what the heck had happened to him. "Let's go upstairs and get dried off."

When we got off the bed, I saw about a quarter inch of standing water on the floor. Hopefully, all this magical moisture won't ruin the finish. I grabbed some towels from the bathroom to soak up the bulk of it, and went upstairs to my bedroom and master bathroom. After I'd shed my clothes and thrown them into the tub, I began blow drying my hair. While I was wondering if Stuart would like his fur blow dried, my gaze moved toward the window, and landed right on Barbara Stevens's house.

"Is Barbara a true victim, or have her past actions come back to haunt her?" I muttered. I'd never gotten a bad vibe from Barbara, but that didn't mean she wasn't doing anything wrong. Good people can still commit the occasional bad act, and something had to have happened to make Francesca suddenly snap. I needed to tell Dan what I'd learned, so we could figure out our next move.

I pulled on my bathrobe and ran downstairs to get my phone. As soon as I found it, I called Dan.

"Hey, baby."

"Francesca Wexford can create glamours but she needs body parts to do it! Also, I had a vision where she admitted to the murders."

"Great. Can't use that in court, though."

"I know. Did you find my blood?"

"No. We think Besami took it."
"Shit."

A Few Problems

I hung up with Eli and glanced at Jacob. "Did you hear all that?"

"I did," Jacob replied. "Interesting that Francesca is choosing to wear her dead brother's lover's face. The fact that it's my sister's face makes it all the more disturbing for me," he added.

"That is creepy," I said. "Let's assume Francesca has Eli's blood. How easy would it be for her to craft a glamour of my wife?"

"It wouldn't be difficult at all, but what concerns me is that she evidently has a piece of my sister," Jacob said. "Granted, it could be something as innocuous as a lock of Cecily's hair, but what if Francesca is collecting trophies from witches she's done away with?"

"That's serial killer behavior right there," I said, then I handed Jacob my phone. "Do me a favor and call Eli? She needs to hear this new theory. Put it on speaker, please."

Jacob did as asked. Eli picked up a moment later. "Tell me you found my blood."

"First, you're on speaker," I said. "Second, get this. We think Francesca's got a piece of Cecily. Jacob's wondering if she's taking trophies."

"And we did think this case looked like a serial killer's M.O.," Eli finished. My girl was smart, sharp, and she was always thinking of the next step. "I'll search for similar cases where victims had parts missing. Good thinking, Jacob."

"Thank you," Jacob said. "We're headed to Bennet's house. Can you think of any reason why Francesca, or the senator, would target him?"

"Bennet's pretty harmless," Eli replied. "But he did propagate the mandrakes that ended up in our crime scene."

Jacob shook his head. "Of course he did. He's always been easily swayed by a pretty face."

"Babe, we're on his street now," I said. "Talk soon."

"Be careful, guys," Eli said.

I ended the call as I pulled up in front of Bennet's house, or should I say cottage. With its dormer windows and overflowing yet orderly flower beds, Bennet's place looked like it had been plucked from the English countryside and set right in the middle of a North American neighborhood. Even the white picket fence and matching porch swing were quaint.

"Here we are," I announced. "Refresh my memory. You and Bennet know each other, right?"

"He certainly knows of me," Jacob replied. "It is a shepherd's duty to record the lineages of seers, witches, and any mortals of note. However, I haven't interacted with Mr. Carrington in some time. They work more closely with seers, usually."

"I wonder why that is," I mused, as I got out of the car.

"It's because witches tend to live a great deal longer than seers," Jacob replied; I hadn't even realized he'd heard me. "What lengthens one's lifespan is magic usage, and, generally speaking, witches are far more magically inclined than seers."

"But didn't Eli's grandmother live for an extraordinarily long time? And her father's over one hundred years old, but he looks like he's in his thirties," I added, because me appearing to be the same age as my father-in-law was just strange.

"As Mistress of Seers, Helena used far more magic than most witches do," Jacob replied. "I always suspected she had witches in her ancestry as well, but that has never been confirmed."

"Eli once mentioned that witches and seers were more alike than different."

"She's correct," Jacob affirmed; like I said, my girl is smart and sharp. "As for Eli's father, Alexander's work as the marksman also brings him in contact with a large amount of magic. The marks he gives seers are nothing more than magical sigils etched into the bearer's skin."

I rubbed the tattoo Eli had given me. It felt like that had happened forever ago, and the process itself had hurt like hell, but I couldn't deny that the tattoo had opened a part of my awareness that had been previously closed off. I'd always had strong intuition, but this tattoo had kicked it into overdrive.

My mother had almost had a heart attack when I told her I'd gotten a tattoo. In her eyes, tattoos were only worn by the criminal element, and never by respectable people like her children. I made a mental note to never be so judgmental with my own kid.

I grinned. Me and Eli were having a kid.

Jacob and I walked up to the porch and knocked. Bennet was his usual flustered self when he opened the door.

"Dan, and Mr. Allwood," Bennet said. "Please, come in. I must say, you just missed Eli and her nurse friend by a few minutes."

I stopped dead. "Eli was not here."

"Yes, she was," Bennet insisted. "She and—Nurse Sanders, that's what she called herself—came here and collected Lillian. They claimed there was a break in the case, and she was needed right away."

I squeezed my eyes shut, and said, "Bennet, we've got a few problems. Nurse Sanders's wife hasn't been able to locate her, and we've got a serial killer with the ability to use people's body parts to make glamours running around town."

"It would appear that the serial killer does indeed have possession of Eli's blood," Jacob added.

Bennet removed his glasses and leaned against the wall. "Oh, dear."

MEMORIES

"You have got to be kidding me."

Dan and I were having our third phone conversation of the past ten minutes. During this call, he told me that someone glamoured to look like me, and either the real Angel Sanders, or someone glamoured to look exactly like Angel, had taken Lillian Stevens from Bennet's place and gone... somewhere. Probably nowhere good. And let's not forget, one of them was wearing my face.

"Tell me about it," Dan said. "Listen, do me a favor give and Jill a call. Have her pick you up, then I want both of you to go to Barbara's place. Either her or that assistant of hers needs to come clean with whatever's been going on around here."

"You only want me to call Jill so she won't yell at you."

"True," he admitted. "However, Jacob put a magical tracker on Besami. Or maybe it was just someone who looked like Besami. Anyway, we're going to follow the trail, and hopefully find Angel that way. Even if we don't find Angel, we might get lucky and figure out where Besami stashed your blood."

"All right," I said, because it was a good plan. "But Jill is going to be pissed."

"I know. Be strong, baby. I love you."

"Love you, too."

Dan ended the call, and I stared at the phone in my hand for a few moments. I sighed, since waiting to perform a difficult task never made it easier, and called Jill.

"Yeah?" she barked into the phone. She was already annoyed. Great.

Nine minutes after I relayed what Dan had told me to Jill, she was pulling into my driveway. I saw her from the front windows and went out to meet her.

"Get in," Jill said. I did, then I sent a spell toward the house to lock the door. "Bennet saw Angel?"

She'd asked me that question twice while we were on the phone. "Bennet saw someone that looked like Angel," I replied. "But we can't be certain of their identity, not while people are running around making glamours."

"And they make them from... from people's bodies?" Jill's voice caught at the end, and her hands trembled on the steering wheel.

"They can be made from things as harmless as locks of hair, so if it was someone wearing a glamour, it doesn't mean that Angel is hurt," I said. "And we don't know if it was her or not. Have you checked her location on your phone?"

"We don't share locations." Jill glanced at me. "That sounded harsher than it should have. We don't share locations because back when we were first dating, if Angel saw me going to a rough neighborhood, or near an active crime scene, she worried so much she made herself sick."

"Love does funny things to you."

Jill sighed. "It sure does."

"You don't have some special police locater device, then?" I asked.

"Eli. This is real life. We're not like cop shows."

"I know." But it would have been cool if they had such a contraption. "Anyway, all signs, and my foresight, are pointing toward Barbara being involved. Whether she's a victim or an accomplice is still a little blurry."

"If you ask me, Bergquist is at the center of this," Jill said, mentioning Megan, Barbara's closed-mouthed assistant, who was at the center of the storm. "She doesn't tell the senator about her sister, she doesn't tell you and Dan she was dating one of the other victims... Wait. The third victim, Arthur. He's Barbara's former brother-in-law?"

"Yeah," I said, as Jill's meaning became clear. "And when we mentioned Artie's name as one of the victims, Barbara didn't react at all, but she immediately confirmed that Jerry Goldman was her accountant." I paused. "I'm not trying to make a case for Barbara's innocence, but her reactions seemed pretty genuine."

"And her ex-husband goes by Besami," Jill murmured. "Maybe the other two used aliases, as well. Anything is possible with these people."

"I hear you."

Jill shook her head. "You're even starting to sound like Dan."

"Maybe I've always sounded like this, and Dan is starting to sound like me," I said, and Jill chuckled. "We're going to find Angel. She's going to be fine. In fact, she's probably just out shopping, or taking a nap."

"Yeah. You're probably right. Angel's fine." Jill's mouth was pressed into a thin line. "She has to be."

When we got to Barbara's, Jill immediately transformed from worried wife to no-nonsense police officer. It was pretty cool, if a bit unnerving.

"Officer Sanders, here to see Senator Stevens," Jill said to the person who opened the door, as she flashed her badge.

"And me," I said, as I waved. "Eliza Lyons. Barbara knows me."

"Please, come in," the man said. "Wait here, if you don't mind. I'll go get her now."

The man disappeared into the house, as Jill and I pretended to admire the artwork in the atrium. "Have you ever seen him before?" Jill asked, jerking her chin toward the man going to fetch Barbara.

"No, but I don't come here that often," I replied, then someone squealed on the second-floor balcony. I looked up, and saw my girl Abby hopping up and down and waving at me.

"Eli," she yelled. "Are you here to see me?"

"I'm here to see your mom, but we can hang out," I called back. "Can you come down?"

"Sure," Abby said, and she began clambering down the stairs.

"That kid really loves you," Jill said.

"What can I say. I'm lovable."

"There you go with another Danism," Jill said, then Abby was galloping toward us.

"Got you," I said, as I grabbed Abby in a bear hug. "How have you been?"

"I'm good," she chirped. "What's a Danism?"

"Well," I began, as I set Abby on her feet, "Do you remember Detective Lyons?" Abby nodded. "His first name is Dan, and Officer Sanders here thinks I talk like him."

"You're a police officer?" Abby asked as she stared at Jill, wide eyed. "That's so cool!"

"It's not bad," Jill demurred. She straightened as Barbara joined us.

"Abby is thinking about becoming a police officer one day," Barbara said. "I would prefer an occupation that doesn't involve firearms, but when do parents ever get what they want?" Abby giggled and hid behind Barbara's legs. "What can I do for the two of you?"

"It's about that case Dan and I are working on," I replied. "Is there someplace we can talk?"

"Of course. Abby, run along," Barbara said, as she patted her shoulder.

"Oooo-kay," Abby said, as she slumped away.

"Such a drama llama," I said.

"A smart drama llama, who hears everything and forgets nothing," Barbara said, as she led us into her office. "Now, what's this about your case?"

"Ma'am, is it correct that you were once married to Jared Besami?" Jill asked.

"Yes," Barbara confirmed. "He hasn't died, too, has he?"

"Not that we're aware of," Jill replied. "However, when you were told that Besami's brother was one of the victims, you claimed you didn't know him."

"That's impossible," Barbara said. "Jared doesn't have any siblings."

"He has two," I said. "Arthur and Francesca Wexford. Although, those names were aliases. Their original surnames were Waterford."

"Waterford," Barbara repeated. "I-I'm not sure how this is relevant to me."

"You don't think it's relevant that while your sister is currently running for mayor, your former brother-in-law is found dead behind City Hall?" Jill asked. "Hanging alongside your accountant, and your assistant's sister?"

"No. That's... that's...." Barbara sat heavily. "Who told you these things? About Jared having siblings, that is."

"Lillian did," I replied. "She said she's stayed close with Francesca over the years. She claimed it really bothered you."

"Well, of course it would, but..." Barbara's words trailed off, then she looked up at us. "But why would it bother me? I don't know anyone named Francesca."

I glanced at Jill. She shook her head slightly; great, she didn't have any ideas, either. On a hunch, I asked, "Do you have a wedding album?"

"Um, yes. I kept it for Abby's sake."

"Can we have a look?" I asked.

"I don't see why not." Barbara went to her bookcase and retrieved the album. She opened it up on the desk, and flipped through the pages. When we got to a photograph of the entire wedding party, she paused.

"Who is that?" I asked, as I pointed to the best man.

"That's..." Barbara squinted. "I can't believe I'm saying this, but I've forgotten his name."

"Okay. Name the bridesmaids for me."

Barbara named all of them, except Francesca. While Barbara played the name game, Jill brought up Arthur and Francesca's identification photos on her phone.

"Ma'am, the two people you've forgotten are Arthur and Francesca Wexford," Jill said, as she showed Barbara the pictures. Barbara's eyes went wide, then she grasped my arm.

"Eli, something is wrong with me," she said, panicked. "I have no memory of these people, yet I must know them. They were in my wedding, for god's sake! What else am I forgetting? What's wrong with me?"

"I don't think anything's wrong with you," I said. "Someone's making you forget, and I bet that someone is your assistant."

Magic Always Knows the Truth

The head of the Allwood clan—who was one of the most powerful witches on the East Coast—and I drove aimlessly around the city as we searched for Besami. Technically, we weren't completely aimless, since our plan was to keep following the magical tracker Jacob had placed on Besami back at the hospital. That had amounted to us going in circles for the last thirty minutes. Now, I'm no witch, but this tracker didn't seem to be working too well.

"Turn here," Jacob said. "The impression is stronger to the left."

"Okay." I surveyed the street. "There's no place to turn for a while. How strong is this impression? Do you think he's in one of these buildings?"

"Unsure," Jacob said. "These trackers have never failed me in the past, but this one is flickering in and out like a light bulb that hasn't been properly screwed in."

"Does that mean something is interfering with your tracker?"

"Most likely." Jacob pulled out his phone, because he was a ghost, a witch, and proficient with modern technology. "I'm calling LeClerc. Perhaps Besami returned to his home."

"Good idea." We finally got to that side street Jacob mentioned earlier, and I made a left. "That impression any stronger over here?"

"It's about the same." Jacob put down his phone and frowned. "Jacques did not answer"

Jacob only referred to LeClerc by his first name when he was worried about him. "Maybe he's driving."

"Perhaps. Ah! He sent a text." Jacob read the message, then continued, "There are people at Besami's home. A man and a woman entered a few hours ago, then two different women left, and returned with a third. He's sending a picture of the three women now."

I heard the ping that announced an incoming text. Jacob glanced at the image, and said, "The women appear to be Angel Sanders, Lillian Stevens, and... and Eli."

"Bastard's wearing my wife's face," I grumbled. "Can he get inside?"

"Apparently not. LeClerc has attempted to enter the house a few times, but something is blocking his entry."

"Shit." I banged the steering wheel with my hand. "Address?"

"He's sending it now." Jacob paused, then announced, "The house is at Thirteen Twelve Arbordale Street."

"You have got to be shitting me."

"Have you been to this location before?"

"Yeah. Our new friend from The Black Hat, Dahlia, rents an apartment there."

I parked on the opposite side of the street from Dahlia's place, and took a moment to think. Like the other homes on the street, the house at Thirteen Twelve Arbordale Street was a big old Victorian mansion. Many of those old homes had been converted into apartments decades ago; some thought it was a shame to lose out on such great architecture, while others saw it as a necessary evil in order to provide affordable housing for college students. I didn't have an opinion either way. I just needed to figure out if Dahlia was in with Francesca Wexford and her insane plans.

On the surface, it would be foolish to assume Dahlia wasn't involved. Our big bad, Francesca, was her employer, and now she was inside the same house where Dahlia rented an apartment. Back in my cop days, I would have labeled Dahlia as an accomplice without a second thought. But I wasn't a cop any longer, and despite all the evidence to the contrary, my gut told me that Dahlia was a good kid. That, and after this past year I'd spent in the supernatural community standing by Eli's side, I understood that appearances could be manipulated down to the smallest detail.

Something in the back of my mind clicked. I opened the calendar on my phone to confirm my dates; Eli and I had solved Jacob's murder last March, eleven short months ago. We didn't become a formal couple until five months after that. Now we were married and handfasted, and we had a baby coming. Time flew by so fast I hardly noticed its passing.

"Eli and I haven't even been together for a year," I muttered.

"What was that?" Jacob asked.

"Nothing. Just reflecting on how much my life has changed since that day I got beat down in your basement." Cecily's goons had kidnapped me as bait to flush out Eli, and kicked the crap out of me in the process.

"As I recall, you did your share of beating, as well," Jacob pointed out.

I laughed shortly; Eli had given me a power boost so I could fight my way past Cecily's thugs, and it worked as advertised. I'm not usually a fighter, but showing those creeps the business side of my fists had been fun. "Yeah. I guess I did."

"And Dan, while I acknowledge that I haven't known you or Eli for most of your lives, I do clearly recall the day we met," Jacob continued. "After you freed my spirit from where it had been imprisoned in that cider barn, I learned that not only had I been rescued by the Mistress of Seers, she also let you, a mortal, make contact with her seer's mark so you could communicate with me."

"I remember," I said. "No offense, but when I realized I was talking to a ghost, I almost passed out."

"Understandable," Jacob replied. "However, my point is that what Eli did should not have worked. You touching her mark shouldn't have allowed you more than the barest glimpse of me, yet you could see and converse with me as easily as Eli herself could. The connection worked because you already had strong feelings for Eli, and she reciprocated. While you two might not have known yet that you were meant to be together, the magic knew."

"Magic always knows the truth," I said, and Jacob nodded. "If that's the case, will magic be able to tell if someone's lying?"

"Is the person in question a mortal?"

"As far as I know, yes."

"Absolutely."

After Jacob sent LeClerc a few texts letting him know of our plan, and LeClerc told us he'd finally gotten inside and was scoping out the first floor, we made a new plan. LeClerc had already confirmed that no one had left the house since the three women had arrived, and I wanted to know exactly who they were. The direct approach is always best in my opinion, so Jacob and I knocked on Dahlia's door.

"Hello?" Dahlia said as she opened it, then she recognized me and smiled. "Hey, Dan. Who's—" She paused, as her gaze skated around the porch.

"Who's what?" I asked.

"Nothing," she said. "I thought I saw someone else out here, but it must have been a trick of the light. What's up?"

"You remember that case Eli and I are working on?" I began, while I was inwardly freaking out. Something—a magical something—was keeping Dahlia from registering Jacob's presence. Whatever Francesca was cooking in this house was rapidly getting out of control. "We tracked some of the people involved to this address."

"Here?" Dahlia demanded, a hint of fear in her tone. "How is that possible? Is Eli with you?"

"She's not," I replied. "Do you know who lives in the other apartments?"

"Um, no. I got this place through an agency. The rest of the tenants are quiet, and I've never actually seen them."

"But you have heard them?" I pressed. "There are people living here, right? Or is the rest of the place vacant?"

"There are other renters." Dahlia stepped back behind the threshold. "Dan, I'm a little weirded out here."

I took a step back. While I have been known to come on too strong, Dahlia's perceptions were being manipulated by whatever magic was drenching the property. "I'm sorry. Sometimes when I'm chasing a lead, I get caught up in the moment. Have a good day, Dahlia."

I turned and walked down the steps as Dahlia retreated indoors. "That did not go well," I said to Jacob.

"The home might be warded to make the occupants wary of visitors," Jacob said. "It may be woven into the spell that's disrupting myself and LeClerc, a side effect of that spell, or something else entirely."

"Great." We got back to my truck and got inside. "What we need is a way to get inside that house, and figure out what's happening. Since you and LeClerc are out of commission, I was hoping Dahlia would help us out."

"But she rapidly became terrified of you," Jacob said. "She's never expressed fear toward you before?"

"No. We got along pretty well, up until five minutes ago," I said, as I pulled out my phone.

"Who are you calling?" Jacob asked. "Eli?"

"Nope. I am bringing in the one witch I'm certain can take down whatever Francesca's got going on here," I replied, as I hit call. "Tessa."

FORGETTING

Now that we knew at least two people had been removed from Barbara's memory, we had new questions to answer. Had Barbara forgotten any-one—or anything—else? And how were her memories taken in the first place?

"If someone's taking my memories, does that mean they—these people—do they now know what I-I used to know?" Barbara asked. "Do they have access to legislation I'm working on, passwords, or family... family information?"

"I really don't think so," I soothed. "We'll know for sure once we figure out how this is happening, but transferring memories from one brain to another is almost impossible."

"Almost?" Barbara demanded. "Then it is possible."

"It is, but I've only ever heard of a memory removal being attempted on a deceased brain." Barbara gasped and Jill looked nauseous, but this wasn't the time to sugarcoat things. "Being that you're alive and well, we can rule that out."

"Okay." Barbara smoothed down her skirt, then she adjusted the cuffs of her blouse. Just like that, the no-nonsense senator was back in action. "As long as no one is using my mind against me, I can always re-learn what they took. How do we stop this?"

"That's a great question," I muttered, as I mentally ran down what I knew about magically influencing someone's memory. It wasn't much, but at least I had a starting point. "We probably aren't dealing with a spell."

"A spell?" Barbara asked.

"The people involved seem to be using witchcraft to a certain degree." I hedged. Barbara was trustworthy, but I never revealed supernatural connections when I didn't have to. "Or at least, they want people to think witchcraft is involved."

"Eli," Jill prompted, while Barbara mulled things over. "Why don't you think a spell is involved?"

"So far, everyone connected with this case is mortal, and they don't understand how witchcraft works," I replied. "None of them appear to have any training in true spell work. They're working off witch-based stereotypes, like the legend about mandrakes growing beneath a hanged man."

"About the mandrakes," Jill said. "I know you took one from my crime scene."

"Guilty," I replied. "Want it back?"

Jill's eyes narrowed. "Yes."

"Is this plant what's making me forget my former relatives?" Barbara interjected. "Ladies, let's focus."

"Barbara's right," I said; I knew Jill was meticulous about her crime scenes, but me taking one plant was beside the point. "Since a spell is unlikely, we need to look for a charm. Where do you spend most of your time?"

"Here, in my office," Barbara replied.

"Who else comes in here?" Jill asked.

"Everyone on my team has access to this room," Barbara replied.

I turned in a slow circle, looking for anything that might be a memory charm. "Is anything in here new, or unfamiliar?"

"Other than some paperwork, no," Barbara began, then her gaze landed on the bookcase. "That bookend is new."

I followed her line of sight, and saw a large fluorite crystal sitting on the bookshelf. "This is a little new age-y for you," I said, as I walked over to the shelf. The crystal was about six inches long and two inches wide, and was sitting in a shallow dish of salt.

"This is hilarious," I said, as I picked up the crystal. "Fluorite aids memory, and someone stuck it in salt as if that would short circuit its influence. It's like they wanted to reverse what the crystal was good for."

"It seems to have worked," Barbara said.

"But it shouldn't have." I turned the crystal over, expecting to see a spell scratched into the base. Instead, I saw the number two.

If there was a number two, there had to be a number one, but you wouldn't number just two items. That meant there was a network of at least three memory-altering crystals in Barbara's house. My foresight sparked, letting me know I was correct.

"There are more of these crystals in the house," I said. "They've used these to make a perimeter, which means that your memories are only affected while you're inside of it. As in, you only forget things while you're home. Since you usually work from your home office, these memories are gone most of the time."

"And when you leave, you would suddenly remember that you'd forgotten something," Jill deduced. "We need to fan out and find the rest."

"I've a better idea," Barbara said, as she hit a button on her intercom. "I'll ask the cleaning staff to locate them."

Barbara's cleaning staff was as efficient as the rest of her employees. It took them less than an hour to sweep the entire estate, and turn up seven additional fluorite crystals, each of which were nestled in their own saucer of salt. Three were found on the first floor, three on the second, and one was at the top of the third floor staircase. That one was the crystal holding the entire charm together.

"You see how the others have numbers on the bases, but this one has names etched into the bottom," I said, as I turned them all upside down, and indicated the one with the writing. "The caster wanted you to forget Francesca Wexford, Arthur Wexford..." I squinted, then read and re-read the next part.

"And who, Eli?" Barbara prompted.

"Not a who, but a what." I turned the base around so Barbara and Jill could read it, as well. "They wanted you to forget that Megan Bergquist ever dated Jerry Goldman."

Barbara gasped as Jill radioed the station. "I need a BOLO on one Megan Bergquist," Jill said. "Suspect is involved in the City Hall homicides but unsure to what degree. Assume she's armed and approach with caution."

"You think Megan's armed?" Barbara asked.

"She has placed items in your home that have altered your memory, and concealed both information and evidence in a murder investigation," Jill replied. "I don't think she's harmless."

"What she is, is desperate," I said. "The whole time she's been hiding her involvement. I don't think I want to call her a murderer, not yet, anyway, but she did something, and she doesn't want us to find out what it was." I faced Barbara. "Did Megan come to work today?"

"I'll call security and find out." Barbara made the call as Jill and I stepped away.

"There's something else happening here," Jill said. "It's not adding up."

"It's not," I said, then my foresight sparked so intensely heat shot down my arm like lightning. The heat coalesced into an image in my mind's eye of a cute kid with freckles sprinkled across her nose.

I spun around, and demanded, "Barbara. Where's Abby?"

POP THAT GLAMOUR

Tessa readily agreed to help Jacob and me gain access (those were her words; I asked if she wanted to break into a witch hunter's basement) to the house on Arbordale Street, where Francesca Wexford might be holed up, and Angel might be a captive. What Tessa didn't mention was that since her car was still parked in my driveway, she was walking over.

"Hey," I called out the window, as soon as I saw her and Alex hoofing it at the end of the street. I got out of the truck, and continued, "I would have picked you up."

"It was only a block," Tessa demurred. "Hello, Jacob."

"Greetings, Contessa, Alexander," Jacob said, as he dipped his chin. "Thank you for agreeing to assist us. Normally I would be able to gain entry to any home with ease, but something in or around the property is interfering with my current state."

"Really," Alex said. "Do you feel any differently?"

"Not now, but I think that's because I'm across the street," Jacob replied. "However, when I was standing on the porch I seemed to flicker in and out of reality. The mortal who opened the door couldn't even register my presence. It seems to be affecting LeClerc, as well."

"Interesting," Alex murmured, in a way that reminded me of Eli. "If you start feeling off, let me know at once. I don't want either of you slipping away before you're ready."

"Of course, Marksman," Jacob replied. While it didn't surprise me that Jacob spoke to Alex and Tessa with respect, it reminded me that the supernatural community had an intricate hierarchy unlike anything in modern mortal society. As the marksman, Alex was one of the most powerful individuals in the entire supernatural community, and was only outranked by a few witches, and his own daughter, Eli.

Sometimes, it bothered me that as a mortal, I was at the bottom of the ladder. Most of the time, like right now, I was glad I had friends in high places.

"Who do we think is inside the house?" Tessa asked, as Alex checked out the property.

"Francesca Wexford and Lillian Stevens," I replied. "They may be keeping Angel Sanders here against her will. Also, they're using glamours and one of them is wearing Eli's face."

"If they're wearing glamours, then we really don't know who we're dealing with," Tessa pointed out.

"The perimeter is also warded," Alex said. He'd extended his hand as if he was feeling magical currents flow past him in the air. "That's probably what's affecting you, Jacob, but I don't think that's the ward's purpose."

"What is the purpose?" I asked.

"Could be anything," Alex replied. "It feels thin, as if the caster didn't have enough power to realize their full intent. Most likely, they just wanted the neighbors to overlook anything out of the ordinary, and resist speaking to outsiders, so they wouldn't be interrupted."

"That would explain a lot," I said, recalling how my presence had scared the daylights out of Dahlia. "So how do we pop these glamours and figure out what's really going on?"

Tessa raised an eyebrow at my wording. "In order to reveal that which is true, first we must change our point of view."

"Is it poetry night," I began, then Tessa rubbed her hands together until wisps of smoke drifted upward from her palms.

"The smoke will obscure everything false and otherwise magically affected," Tessa said, as the smoke wafted toward the house. "Once it dissipates, only what's true will remain."

"Wait," Alex said, as he jogged toward the lawn. "I'll reinforce the ward, so the smoke stays close to the house. That way, we can concentrate the magic where it's needed most."

"Good thinking, Alex," Tessa said. "Dan, Jacob, let's also get inside the ward so we're not visible to the neighbors."

That was a good idea, so we all crossed the street and lined up on the lawn like toy soldiers. Once we were all in place, Alex completed a few gestures, then a gold perimeter lit up around the edge of the property line.

"That line is the ward?" I asked.

"Yes," Jacob replied. "I must say, Alexander is almost too powerful for it. See how the border is cracking apart near where he's standing?"

"Yeah," I said, then the smoke began to swirl around the house like a tiny hurricane. As soon as the house was engulfed, Alex clapped his hands, and the ward cracked like an egg, with the perimeter line shattering into gold dust. With nothing left to contain it, Tessa's magic smoke drifted away like fog burning off in the morning sun.

"And now both the glamour and the ward have been dealt with," Tessa announced.

Jacob's phone pinged. "LeClerc is now inside the house," he announced. "He reports that all three mortals are present."

"Should we follow him inside?" I asked, then sirens blared as fire trucks and police cruisers swarmed onto the street. "Shit, I bet someone thought the place was on fire."

"But the smoke was inside the ward, as were we," Tessa said. "No one else would have known what was happening."

"Someone figured it out," I said, as first responders swarmed onto the street.

"Daniel Lyons," a cop barked right behind my head. I turned and regarded the kid, then I remembered him; Jimmy Calloon. He came on the force about a year, year and a half ago.

"Yeah, Calloon?" I asked.

"We got a call from the homeowner saying you were harassing her, and when she wouldn't let you inside, you set a fire out here," Jimmy replied. "What, you leave the force to be a criminal?"

"Calloon, that is not what's happening here," I said, while the rational part of my mind wondered how the cops had gotten here so fast. The ward had literally just cracked, and the station was at least a twenty-minute drive from here... then I saw Dahlia watching everything from the front window. Fricken' magic ruins the day again.

"Let me call my wife," I said.

"Call her from the station," Calloon said, then he grabbed my wrist and slapped a handcuff on me. "Got any weapons I need to know about?"

"Not on me," I replied, then I twisted around and found Eli's father. "Alex, can you call Eli for me? I'm gonna need some bail money."

LIFE'S LAST GIFT

We searched the entire house, basement to attic, east wing to west.

We checked all the security feeds. Not one of them had a recent image of Abby.

Abby was gone. Worse, there was no sign of Megan, either.

"They might not be together," Barbara kept repeating. "Megan wasn't supposed to be here today. Something else could be happening here."

"You're right," I said, even though we hadn't been able to raise Megan via phone or text, and the cruiser Jill sent by Megan's place reported that it was dark and apparently unoccupied. But Barbara did have a point, and we shouldn't fixate on Megan being responsible for Abby's disappearance and possibly overlook the actual suspect.

"Let's talk this through," I said. "Who else would have taken Abby? What about her father?"

"Jared?" Barbara scoffed. "Doubtful. We haven't seen Jared in years. I don't know if he's even in the area."

That was not what I was expecting to hear. "I just saw Jared at the hospital," I said. "I was in the emergency room, and he was my doctor. He gave me an ultrasound."

"Jared is a neurosurgeon," Barbara said. "He wouldn't lower himself to work a shift in the ER or to do a tech's job."

I stared at Barbara for a moment, then I looked over my shoulder, and yelled, "Jill!"

"What happened?" Jill demanded, as she jogged back inside; the police had formed a staging area in Barbara's driveway. It was eerily familiar to the scene from three years ago, when Abby was last kidnapped.

"The Jared Besami Dan and I encountered at the hospital may have been an imposter," I said. "According to Barbara, he's a surgeon."

"*Neuro*surgeon," Barbara clarified. "He's one of the best on the east coast."

"And neuros don't do grunt work," Jill muttered. She knew all about how hospitals operated, since Angel was a registered nurse. Jill rubbed her eyes, and asked, "When Abby was taken before, how did that shake out? What was the prime motive?"

"Money," Barbara replied. "The kidnappers didn't know me or Jared personally. They only wanted to ransom her."

Jill blew out a breath. "The person we need on this is Dan. No offense, Eli, but Dan is the best detective I've ever met."

"None taken." I pulled out my phone and called Dan. It went straight to voice mail.

"I don't know about that, Officer Sanders," Barbara said. "Dan is quite capable, but Eli is the one that brought my girl home."

"That had less to do with skill than me using resources Dan did not have," I said, as I hit call again. Straight to voice mail, again. "He's not picking up."

"Great," Jill grumbled. "Add him to the list of missing people." Her phone rang just as mine chirped. Assuming Dan was calling me back, I answered immediately.

"Where are you?" I demanded.

"Bug, we have a problem," my dad said.

"We have a lot of them," I replied, surprised and somewhat relieved to hear my father's voice. "Do you know where Dan is?"

"That's why I'm calling. He's been arrested for stalking."

"What?" I squeaked.

"They're putting him in the cruiser now."

"Stop them," I shrieked. "Don't let them take him away!"

"How am I supposed to do that?" he demanded.

"Do whatever you have to! Where is this happening?"

"We're on Arbordale Street," he replied, then I heard him call Tessa's name. "Don't let them take Dan anywhere," he told her.

"Let me guess, you're at Dahlia Evergreen's place?" I asked.

"Yes. Tessa's talking to the officers now. Dan isn't in the car yet."

"Keep everyone there," I said. "I'm on my way."

I ended the call with my father as Jill ended hers. "Dan's been arrested," I said.

"Yeah," Jill said. "Chief just called. He's also being charged with arson."

"What is happening," I mumbled; we were used to things being crazy, but this was just nuts. I glanced at Barbara, who was understandably beside herself over Abby's second kidnapping, but I needed to go to Dan, and Jill still had to find Angel, and—

Wait. This was the second time Abby had been kidnapped. What were the odds of that?

"Barbara, was Megan working for you when Abby was taken before?" I demanded. "And what about Jerry Goldman?"

"Why, yes, they both were," she replied. "Megan and Jer had just started dating... Eli, I'm starting to remember things."

"Wonderful." I turned to Jill. "How many random-seeming kidnappings are actually random?"

"Very few," Jill replied. "You're thinking that Megan was involved in both of Abby's abductions?"

"Yes," I replied. "Lillian claimed that Jerry was skimming funds from his clients. Someone with full access to this house has put forgetting charms all over the place, and someone—possibly the same person responsible for the charms—just whisked Abby out of here right past all of this high-tech security and cameras. Megan would know how to bypass all of that, wouldn't she?"

"And Megan's been lying since the beginning," Jill said, before Barbara could defend her assistant. "I'll tell the lead officer we have a possible suspect. Wait here." I watched Jill return to the knot of police officers outside, all the while wondering how soon I could leave Barbara's house and help Dan.

"Eliza."

Barbara's tone reminded me of a middle school teacher who'd long since had enough. "Yeah?"

"Where did you learn about things like forgetting charms?" Barbara asked. "What aren't you telling me?"

"A lot, honestly." I faced her, and laid my cards on the table. "Here's the deal. I'm a private investigator, but I'm also the Mistress of Seers. That means I can talk to the dead."

Barbara shook her head. "That's insane."

"A bit, yeah. But three years ago, a ghost told me where to find Abby, and I bet a ghost can help us now."

"You told me you pulled into that truck stop to get gas, and coincidentally saw Abby!"

"Actually, my ghost friend, Prudence, found the truck they were keeping Abby in," I replied. "She told me where the truck was, and followed it until it stopped and they let her out."

"And you think you can ask this Prudence where Abby is now?"

"No. I'm going to summon Megan's sister, Colleen."

Barbara remained skeptical of my supernatural abilities, but she was willing to go along with a séance if it meant we could locate Abby that much sooner. The person standing in our way was Jill.

"Eli, this is nuts," Jill said. The three of us were standing in the butler's pantry, since it was windowless and had a drawer full of candles. It was much easier to see ghosts in a darkened room lit only by candlelight, as I tried explaining to Officer Skeptic. "I can't be hiding in here taking to ghosts! I have an investigation to run, I still don't know where my wife is, your husband just got arrested—"

"Jill," I said, effectively ending her tirade. "First of all, can we all agree that Abby is our highest priority?"

"Definitely," Barbara said.

"Of course," Jill added, with a nod in Barbara's direction.

"Great." I loved it when everyone got along. "LeClerc—that's Jacob Allwood's assistant," I added, for Barbara's benefit, "also reported seeing Angel at the Arbordale Street house, which is where Dan, my dad, and Tessa and Jacob are currently located. None of them will let anything happen to Angel. You know that."

Jill huffed. She actually huffed at me. "And what about Dan? Who is currently in handcuffs in the back of a cruiser?"

"My father and Tess are making sure the cops won't leave before we get there," I replied.

"Exactly how are they doing that?" Jill asked. "Magically?"

"I have no idea, but they're on it. But my point is that Dan and Angel are in known locations and relatively safe. That means we have a small window of opportunity to focus solely on Abby, so we can find her as soon as possible. Agreed?"

"Yes, agreed," Barbara said. "What do we need to do?"

"Get me a few candles. And do either of you have an ink pen?"

"Why do you need a pen?" Jill asked, as she handed hers over. "Starting your memoirs?"

"Funny. Give me your hand." Jill did, and I sketched a quick image of a sun on her wrist, while I concentrated on opening her awareness to the world beyond the veil. "This is going to be your temporary seer's mark. It will enable you to see Colleen's spirit when I summon her."

"You mean to tell me that the key to seeing ghosts is having you draw on my skin?" Jill asked.

"No. As Mistress of Seers, I can imbue the drawing with enough of my own power to act as a seer's mark until the ink wears off." I showed her the mark on my left wrist. My father tattooed it on me when I was sixteen, although since I'm a seer by birth, I'd already been able to interact with the dead. My mark acted as a power booster to my natural abilities. "See how mine is permanent?"

"Yeah," Jill said. "Does this mean I'm haunted until the mark wears off?"

"I doubt you'll see a single other ghost besides Colleen. Most have better things to do than heckle the living." I finished the sun's rays, and added a smiley face. "I picked a sun for your mark, because you're all sunshine and roses when Angel's in the room."

Jill frowned, then she glanced at the sun and her features softened. "She's always brought out the best in me."

"It's what good spouses do. Barbara?" I held up my pen. "Your turn."

Barbara extended her hand, but she didn't look happy about it. "What will my drawing look like?"

"A bee, because you're so busy." I glanced up, saw her pinched brows. "Hey. This is going to work. We will get Abby back, and get those responsible for taking her put away for a long, long time."

"I hope you're right." She reclaimed her hand, and briefly examined the bumble bee I'd drawn on her skin. Gotta say, it wasn't my best work, but it would have to do. "I'm so worried I can hardly think."

"I know, and we're going to find her. Promise. Let's get the candles set up."

Barbara put a couple of white taper candles into brass candlesticks, and set them on the counter. "Now what?"

I snapped my fingers to light the candles. Barbara gasped; the candle trick always impressed the newbies. As for Jill, she only rolled her eyes. "Now, we just have to wait for Colleen to join us."

"I'm here."

"That was fast," I said, as I turned around and faced Colleen. Her spirit seemed calmer than the last time we encountered each other, which was good. That meant she was settling into her new form.

"Oh, my god," Jill murmured. "A real live ghost."

"She's not alive," I whispered, then I turned back to our spiritual visitor. "Colleen, this is Jill Sanders. She's investigating your death."

"Um, hi," Colleen said. "Got any leads?"

"We do," Jill said. "But Eli asked you here so we could talk about your sister, Megan."

Panic skated across Colleen's face. "Is Megan hurt? Is she in trouble again?"

Barbara cleared her throat, and began, "Megan is my assistant. We think she may have something to do with my daughter's abduction."

"No," Colleen said, shaking her head. "That can't be right. After the mess she got into with the senator's kid, Megan swore she'd never resort to kidnappings again."

With that revelation, Collen shocked us into a silence so profound, you could have heard a pin drop. "Colleen, meet Senator Barbara Stevens," I said, as Colleen's eyes got so wide they looked like ping pong balls protruding from her face. "Also known as the kidnapped girl's mother."

"Oh, shit," Colleen said, as she covered her mouth with her hand. "Ma'am, I'm so sorry your baby got pulled into all of this."

"Can you help us find Abby?" Barbara demanded.

Colleen nodded vigorously. "I will help any way I can."

"You mentioned that Megan was in some kind of a mess," I said. "Do you know what happened there? What made her want to take Abby the first time?"

"It wasn't Megan's fault," Colleen said. "She started dating this skeevy accountant. He was stealing from a few of his clients, but he was worried he was about to get caught."

"Was that accountant Jerry Goldman?" I asked.

"Yeah," Colleen replied. "He's such a scumbag, but he gets away with it because he's two faced, you know? Always acted like the smooth businessman, then he would turn around and blow his client's retirement fund at the casino, or on whatever he was into at the time."

"Do you know who Goldman was stealing from?" Jill asked.

"As far as I know, it was from a few different people. He had a real bad gambling addiction, among all of his other issues." Colleen held her hands out in front of her, fingers spread. "I look so real here."

"You are real," I said. "You will always be yourself, no matter what form you take. A spirit is no less of an individual than a flesh and blood body."

Colleen nodded. "I guess. It's just so weird to be…not alive any more."

"I bet." I glanced at Barbara, and continued, "Colleen, I will help you transition fully to your next form. I swear to you I will help in any way possible, but right now we need to know more about what Megan got involved with, and why they took Abby again."

"She must be so scared," Barbara said, as she dashed her hand across her eyes. "She's only eight."

"I get it," Colleen said, nodding. "But Megan wasn't directly involved in the kidnapping. She gave Jerry a bunch of information about the girl's schedule, and the house's security plan, and he sold the information to some people he owed money to. They were professional kidnappers, and they were going to ransom the girl for a ton of money."

"Those kidnappers are in jail," Jill said. "But it was Megan who facilitated everything?"

"I don't know if facilitated is the word I'd use," Colleen said. "But Megan was desperate, and she knew the kid's family had money." She glanced around the room, and said to Barbara, "I guess she was right about that."

"Money is a poor motivator," Barbara hissed, but Jill held up her hand.

"Were Megan and Jerry the only ones involved, aside from the pros?" Jill asked Colleen.

"No. There was a relative of Abby's, an aunt. She distracted everyone on the day they took the kid."

Barbara's mouth was pressed into a thin line. "I will destroy Lillian for this," she seethed.

"It could have been Francesca," I said.

"Francesca was who Megan and Jerry went to later," Colleen said. "She would sell people spells and charms out of this little storefront in the next town. When Jer got in over his head, he bought a lot of money spells from her." Colleen laughed shortly. "I guess they never worked."

"This was Francesca Wexford that sold these spells?" Jill asked, and Colleen affirmed that it was correct. "Did you know her well?"

"Not really, but she was always nice to me," Colleen replied. "She gave me my first tarot deck."

"Colleen," I began, "your body was found with Jerry Goldman and Artie Wexford. We think Francesca got mad at Artie because he was dating a witch, and we're wondering if she was also upset with Jerry."

"Oh, yeah, Francesca was mad at both of them," Colleen said. "We were all at the old place in Westhampton, and Artie told her... told her..." Colleen shook her head. "I-I can't remember exactly what happened, but it was bad. Francesca flipped out screaming at him, told him he was an ungrateful kid, all sorts of mean stuff. It was really awful."

"I'm sure it was," I said. "Does Francesca have a place anywhere in town, or does she stay out at that storefront you mentioned?"

"She owns one of those three deckers out by the college," Colleen replied. "It's on Arbordale Street." She looked down at herself. "Eliza, I feel like I'm fading."

"It takes a lot of energy to make yourself visible," I said. "You've already been a big help. Can you come find me after you've rested a bit?"

"Yeah, I will," Colleen said, as she faded from view. "See you soon, Eliza."

After Colleen was gone, Barbara blew out the candles and went to open the pantry door. "Why couldn't Colleen remember any more about the fight with Francesca?" Jill asked.

"Pretty sure she was recounting the last few minutes before her death," I replied. "People usually forget the events leading up to their demise, especially if it was violent. My grandmother used to refer to those forgotten memories as life's last gift."

"We got confirmation of who our killer is in the worst way possible," Jill said. "I can't exactly enter a statement gotten from a ghost in a pantry into evidence."

I threw my hands up in the air. "Seriously, Jill? I'm a seer. What kind of help did you think I'd be getting?"

"Help that's admissible in court," Jill snarked back. "But it sounds like Abby's also on Arbordale Street with the rest. I'll tell the guys out front that they should stay here, and we're going to check out a lead."

"Good," Barbara said. "And as soon as I get Abby safe, I am going to wring Lillian's neck!"

A Literal Circus

I'd definitely had better days.

After Calloon got the cuffs on me—an act he enjoyed a little too much, if you ask me—Tessa came over to inquire as to why I was being detained. At first, Calloon was so taken with Tessa's old-world charms he forgot all about me, and left me standing next to the cruiser like a potted plant. However, what Calloon failed to realize was that Tessa knew more about the law than he ever would.

"I still don't understand why you're arresting Dan," Tessa said. "You came out here based on a complaint of stalking, but what makes you think Dan is the suspect? Where is the complainant, and where is her statement?"

"The caller mentioned Lyons by name," Calloon said. "That's all the evidence I need."

"It's not," I said. "Any rookie knows that. And why would I be out here stalking some other woman with my father-in-law? That's a pretty weak case, even for you."

"Shut it, Lyons," Calloon snapped. "I've had enough of you. For months now I've been listening to the chief whine about how he lost his best detective, then you go and shack up with that freaky hot woman—"

I was in his face in a hot second. "What was that about my wife?"

"I said what I said," Calloon snapped back. "What that chick sees in your sorry ass is a mystery."

I stepped closer. "Take these cuffs off me and say that again. Better yet, I'll beat the stupid out of you with them on."

"Try it," Calloon sneered. "They I get to bring you in for assaulting an officer."

"Perhaps we shouldn't assault anyone," Alex said. "Officer Calloon, you were explaining the nature of the complaint that the resident called in to the station?"

Calloon started babbling at Alex, but I ignored him. Just as I turned to Tessa, intending to ask her to use some magic to get these cuffs off me, Jill's car screeched to a halt next to mine.

"We've got a situation in the house," Jill announced, as she, Barbara Stevens, and Eli filed out of the car. "Calloon, why is Lyons in cuffs? Get him loose. Now!"

"Sanders, you can't—" Calloon spluttered.

"Do. It. Now," Jill repeated. "We've got reports of two kidnapping victims inside this house, one of which is a minor. Get your head out of your ass and make yourself useful."

Calloon was still staring at Jill when Eli ran up to me. "Megan Bergquist took Abby," Eli said, as she touched my cuffs. A second later, they fell to the ground, and I was holding my girl. "I summoned Colleen's ghost. Megan and Jerry Goldman were behind Abby getting taken before, and I'm pretty sure Francesca killed all three of our victims."

"All right," I said; I wanted to keep holding Eli, but Abby came first. "Who's else have they got in there?"

"Angel."

I glanced at Jill, saw her issuing orders like a general in battle. "Shit. All right, it might not be as bad as it seems. LeClerc's on the inside, keeping an eye on things. Jacob just went to get an update from him. Come on." I scooped up the handcuffs from where they'd fallen, then I took Eli's hand and began walking toward Jill. On the way, I dropped the cuffs in Calloon's hands. Let him take his sweet ass time figuring out how I got loose. "Dahlia's in there, too."

"So we have three innocents." Eli glanced around the property. "And this is a literal circus. No way Francesca doesn't know we're out here."

"Not necessarily," Tessa said, as she joined us. "Maintaining a glamour takes a great deal of energy. Francesca may be too weak to sense what's happening outside. She may even be catatonic after such extended use."

"It would explain why the ward was so fragile," Alex added, then he explained the ward, and how he and Tess had disarmed it, to Eli.

"So the question becomes, should we sneak the innocents out of the house, or take out the bad guys first?" Eli mused.

"Normally, I'd say we negotiate with the person in charge," I said. "But this is far from normal. Sanders?"

Jill turned around. "Angel's in there," she said.

"Then she can look out for Abby," I said. "Angel's tough, way tougher than you, and you know she won't let anyone hurt a kid. Don't forget that."

"While she's being tough, we need to set a perimeter around the house," Jill ordered. "Get the neighboring houses evacuated, and we need to get someone inside. Someone living," Jill added, with a meaningful look toward Eli.

"I'll go," Eli volunteered. "I've got my protection bubble, and I can work with Jacob and LeClerc. We can get everyone out, and let you guys know what you're dealing with."

Jill nodded. "Go."

"Wait," I said. "I'm going with you."

Eli grasped my hand. "Let's do it."

We stood together, facing the house. On our left was a driveway and a detached garage, straight ahead was the front porch with doorways that led to different apartments, and on the right was a small, fenced-in yard. "Which way should we go?" Eli asked.

"Doubtful they're in the garage," I began. "When you want to hide what you're doing, ground level is a no-go. They're either in the basement, or the attic."

"Let's go around the side, and see if there's a basement door," Eli said. "If they aren't down there, we can work our way up."

"Lead the way, babe."

We started walking across the snow-crusted lawn on the right side of the house. All I could see on that side were a few overgrown shrubs, but no doorway. Eli was investigating the fence that cordoned off the backyard when Dahlia came running toward us.

"Dan, I'm so sorry I called the cops," she yelled. "I don't know why I did that!"

"It's all right," I said. "Magic makes us screwy sometimes. See Jill over there?" I pointed toward the police presence in the road. "Go tell her everything you know."

Dahlia nodded. "Okay, I'll do that now."

"Oh, and where's Francesca?"

"She's beneath you," Dahlia said.

"Beneath?" I assumed she meant the basement. "Is there an outside door?"

The ground shook, and I looked at Eli. "Earthquake?"

"No," Francesca said, as she erupted from the ground and grabbed me.

Shit.

Was I buried alive?

THE TROPHY WALL

"What the hell was that?" I shrieked. A woman shot up out of the ground, grabbed Dan, then both of them disappeared back into the dirt. There wasn't even a hole left behind.

I dropped to my knees and clawed at the ground. The snow on top of the lawn wasn't disturbed, except for where I shoved it aside. The ground beneath was frozen, and unbroken, and beneath it was dead grass and frozen soil. Dan had completely disappeared.

What the hell had Francesca done with my husband?

I scrambled to my feet and grabbed Dahlia's shoulders. "Where is Dan?" I demanded. "Where did she take him?"

"It was Francesca," Dahlia said. "She made me come out here!"

I yanked Dahlia closer, until we were nose to nose. "I don't care what she made you do. Where is my husband?"

"I'm so sorry," Dahlia blubbered, and it was all I could do not to smack her.

"Feel guilty later," I said. "Where does Francesca work? The kitchen, or maybe in the garage?"

"The b-basement," Dahlia said.

Finally, useful information. "How do I get down there?"

"There's an access door in the back. It's where Francesca keeps people, living and dead."

My blood went cold. "Are there any dead people down there now?"

"I-I don't know," Dahlia said, then she started bawling. "I'm so sorry."

"Do what Dan said. Go to Jill." I couldn't rescue Dan or anyone while she was crying all over me. "I'm going in."

I left Dahlia to her meltdown, and hopped the low fence into the backyard. I took a moment to orient myself, and noted the shed in the far corner of the property, the row of yew bushes that had likely been planted as a privacy hedge, and the rusted out bulkhead against the back wall of the house. Looked like that was my way inside.

When I got closer to the bulkhead, I noticed a padlock sealing it shut. No big, I could handle a simple lock, but Francesca's leap out of the dirt and subsequent disappearance made me pause. For her to snatch Dan like that, and then vanish so completely, she must be a lot more powerful than we'd realized.

I leaned against the house as a wave of guilt and sadness washed over me. Dan was somewhere underground, trapped and possibly hurt, and I hadn't even sensed Francesca's approach. So much for my heightened foresight, and all my seer and witchy abilities. Yet again, I'd failed at keeping the person I loved most safe.

"Okay," I said, as I shook out my hands. "Pity party's over. Let's get everyone home." I closed my eyes, and summoned Jacob.

"Finally," Jacob said, when he materialized in front of me. "Eli, things are not good in that house."

"Tell me everything," I said. "Is there a young girl in the basement?"

"Abby? Yes, she arrived with Megan," Jacob said. "They aren't in the basement. Lillian is keeping Abby occupied in one of the second floor apartments, and Megan appears to regret her actions."

"Nice of her to grow some morals," I muttered. "Have you seen Dan?"

Jacob's face darkened. "He's in the laboratory, with Angel. They're both relatively unharmed. LeClerc is watching them, and so far no one has detected him or myself."

"That's the best news I've heard all day. Can you tell Officer Sanders where Abby is, so they can get her out?"

"I'm not sure I can," Jacob said. "Ever since LeClerc and I arrived at this property, we've felt ourselves slipping away. Mortals may not be able to notice me."

I gasped; it sounded like Jacob was finally moving to the other side, and LeClerc was right behind him. In the year since we met, I'd grown to rely on Jacob in many ways, and I wasn't ready to say goodbye. "How do you feel? Are you passing over? Is that what you want?"

"I don't feel any different," he replied. "There was a hastily crafted ward on the house. We suspect it may have contributed to my and LeClerc's present condition."

"Okay, let's hope your present condition is due to the ward," I said. "My father's over there with the rest. He'll be able to see you, regardless of what the ward did or didn't do to you."

Jacob nodded. "Shall I tell him your plans?"

"I'm going into the basement." I jerked my chin toward the padlock. "Do we think that's charmed in any way?"

Jacob waved his hand over the lock. "It appears to be a mundane lock. I'll return to you after Abby's free."

"Sounds like a plan."

As Jacob walked toward the police presence out front, I crouched down and studied the lock; now that Jacob had assured me that everyone was safe, I could take my time getting inside the place. That extra bit of caution might be the only thing keeping me from ending up as Francesca's next victim. But first, I needed to conquer this lock.

Back in the day, I would have pulled out my lock picks in order to break in. Now that I knew I was half witch, and understood my abilities better than ever, I merely touched the old rusted metal. A moment later, the lock popped open.

"Thank you," I whispered, then I hauled the bulkhead doors open. The interior was dark and musty, and smelled like damp earth. I had the overwhelming feeling of walking into a grave. Here's hoping it wasn't my own.

"It's okay, buddy," I said, as I rested my hand on my belly. "We're just going to get Daddy, then Auntie Angel, then we'll be out of here. Sound good?" Unsurprisingly, the baby was silent on the matter. I took a last breath of fresh air, and descended into the basement.

Once I was down there, I realized the basement had a dirt floor. That wasn't so unusual, at least not in this part of the country, where many houses had been built over a century ago with root cellars for overwintering produce. What was unusual were the dirt walls, and the massive roots dangling from the ceiling.

It's like someone dug a pit underneath the house. In addition to the dirt décor, the only light in the room was what filtered down from the open bulkhead. I crept deeper into the basement, pushing aside lengths of moss and cobwebs as I went. Eventually, I reached a cinderblock wall. I felt my way along the wall in the deepening darkness, until I found a door, and then a handle. Hoping I wasn't about to walk into something worse, I turned the knob.

And entered a laboratory.

"I was not expecting this," I muttered. The room still had dirt walls and a root-encrusted ceiling, but stainless steel tables and various types of equipment were set up along the length of the walls. Overhead fluorescent lighting bathed everything in sterile white light. On the tables were various glass flasks and test tubes, and I even saw a Bunsen burner at the far end.

"Is someone recreating a high school science lab?" I muttered.

"If only it was that simple," Angel said, as she stepped out from the shadowed corner. "Eli, is it really you?"

"Of course," I said, then I remembered how she'd been picked up by someone wearing my face. "How can I prove it? I know all these glamours are nuts."

"What is Jill's middle name?" she asked.

"I have no idea," I replied. "However, I do know that Dan is forbidden from ever speaking it again. The story is that she dumped a bowl of potato salad on him when he said it before."

"Actually, it was egg salad," Angel said, then she pulled me in for a hug. "Eli, I am so glad to see you."

"Same," I said, as she squeezed the life out of me. "Are you okay? Jill's outside."

"My Jilly," Angel said. "And yeah, I'm fine. As for Dan... Well, come have a look."

I froze in place. "Is he hurt?"

"I'm really not sure." Jill drew me toward the door on the opposite side of the lab room, and cracked it open. My heart in my throat, I peered into what appeared to be the main room of the basement. It had the same dirt walls and harsh overhead lighting as the lab, but the floor was covered in plastic sheeting, and there were large wooden boxes shoved against one wall.

Those boxes were the right size and shape for coffins.

As for Francesca, she was pacing the room like a caged tiger, and she was alone. That was the only good thing happening in that room.

"Where's Dan?" I whispered to Angel. She pointed straight ahead. I followed her gaze, and almost choked.

Dan was upright with his back pressed against the far wall, and his arms and legs sunken into the dirt.

Angel dragged me away from the door, and hissed, "Quiet. Francesca not knowing you're down here is our only advantage."

"No, we have another," I said, then I summoned LeClerc. He appeared almost instantly, and scared the crap out of Angel.

"Angel, this is LeClerc," I said. "He's been watching over all of you."

"Apologies for startling you," LeClerc said.

"It's fine," Angel said, as she fanned herself. "Just the latest strange thing to happen today."

"Typical day around these parts," I said, as I squeezed her hand. "Based on the fact that Angel can see you, I'm guessing whatever was screwing with you and Jacob is wearing off?" I asked LeClerc.

"Evidently so," he replied. "The young girl is safe upstairs. As for Dan's current situation, Francesca has developed some rather concerning abilities."

"Power over the earth?" I asked, and he nodded. I recalled my vision of Francesca and her brothers stashed in the bunker. "Do you think her abilities are based in trauma? Her father was a serial killer, and kept the kids trapped underground."

"I suppose it's possible," LeClerc said. "What I find more concerning is what she had Angel doing in this room."

"Were... were you watching me?" Angel demanded, aghast.

"Only enough to ensure your safety," LeClerc replied diplomatically.

"What's the lab for?" I demanded, like the uncouth barbarian I am.

"She wants me to synthesize some form of essence from these assorted body parts." Angel beckoned us to a tall shelving unit. On the lower shelves were various bones and tufts of hair. The upper shelves had bottles of liquid, and items bobbing in them that looked suspiciously like flesh and other dissected body parts.

I gagged, then I ran to the opposite corner and puked. "Sorry, guys."

"Don't worry about it," Angel said. "This is beyond repulsive. Francesca had a notebook with lists of who these specimens came from, and wanted me to extract magical powers from them. I almost told her there was no way I could do that, but I didn't want to anger the crazy woman."

"Smart. Actually, we can use that notebook to prove she's a serial killer," I said. "That, and her gross trophy wall."

"I've got the notebook," Angel said, as she pulled it out of her back pocket. "Jill likes things to be admissible in court, and I believe this fits the bill."

"It sure does," I said. "I don't suppose you found my blood lying around this hellhole?"

Angel withdrew a vial from her other pocket and handed it to me. "Got it right here. But Eli, there are people besides Dan in the next room. One of them is Jared Besami."

"Is he alive?"

"Barely," Angel replied. "She's keeping him just this side of dead, though I can't imagine why. She wouldn't let me treat him, or even make him comfortable."

"She's been impersonating him," I said. "Francesca figured out how to use people's body parts to copy their appearance."

"That was how she looked like you," Angel said. "Gotta say, after she reverted to her actual face, I was questioning my sanity."

"I bet." I went back to the door and looked at Dan. His eyes were closed, but I could see his chest rising and falling. "LeClerc, can you let Dan know I'm here?"

"Of course," LeClerc said, as he faded from view.

"Was that... Is he a ghost?" Angel asked.

"Correct," I replied, then Jacob appeared. "And so is he."

"Officers are about to breach the home," Jacob began, then we heard a crash upstairs. "Now."

"That means Abby's safe," I said, as I turned back toward Dan. "Now the rest of us need to get out."

DOWN IN THE DIRT

I was dirty.

No, no. That's not right.

I am in dirt.

Confused and filthy, I went over my most recent memories. A woman had appeared in front of me, then I fell. At first, I thought I'd taken a step back and stumbled into a hole, but I hadn't ended up at the bottom of anything. I was upright, and I was in a wall, and that wall was made of dirt.

What the hell was happening here?

Slowly, I moved my head back and forth. Dry clods of soil fell away from the sides of my face and my forehead. That's when I realized this wasn't just dirt. It was mud.

Fricken' great.

I pulled my arms forward, and got nowhere. Whatever this mud was made of, it was heavy and dense, much like my head for letting my guard down while we were talking to Dahlia. That kid had a lot of explaining to do, and as soon as I found Eli—

My eyes snapped open, and a ton of debris fell in them. I blinked until my vision was clear, and scanned the room. I couldn't see or hear Eli, which hopefully meant she hadn't gotten dragged down alongside me. That was good. What wasn't good was the stack of coffins in the corner, and the stench of decay.

"Is anyone here?" I yelled. A door opened up, and a woman stood silhouetted in light. "Where's my wife?"

"You mean the witch?" the woman who I assumed was Francesca countered. "I only had time to grab you. Don't worry, I'll cleanse you of her influence."

"Cleanse?" I repeated. Behind Francesca, I saw Angel. She didn't look hurt, but her eyes were wide and her hands were clenched in a knot. "If you want to clean me up, why did you dump me in all this dirt?"

Francesca didn't bother responding to me. Instead, she said to Angel, "Keep working. I want to know when you have results."

"What's she working on?" I asked, as Francesca shut the door. Now it was me, her, and a bunch of corpses. "And who are all those people in the corner? More witches?"

"More people who got in my way," she replied. "Are you planning on getting in my way?"

"Not if I'm stuck in this wall."

Francesca chuckled, then she moved toward the far corner of the room. She turned on a lamp, and I saw an old recliner. I could see a head above the top edge of the chair. Before I could ask who was in it, she spun the chair around and revealed Jared Besami.

"That your brother?" I asked.

"Yes. This is the legendary Jared, he who saved us from our living tomb, and got our father sent to prison."

"He doesn't look so good." Jared's skin was sallow and his eyes were sunken into his skull. I wasn't entirely sure he was alive. "Maybe we should call an ambulance."

"Jared doesn't need an ambulance. All he needs is me." She stroked her brother's face in a far too intimate manner. "What Jared never realized was that Father was right. Underground was safe." She shook her head. "We never should have left."

"Is that what's happening here?" I asked. "Bunker number two?"

"No. This is my laboratory." She gestured toward the room Angel was in with a flourish, as if we weren't stuck at the bottom of a glorified hole. "It's where I work out my own spells."

"How is that any different that what a witch does?" I asked. Behind Francesca, LeClerc appeared. He pointed toward the laboratory's door, then he was gone. I took that to mean something was happening, and to keep Francesca distracted. "Seems like you're jealous of all these witches."

"Jealous?" she demanded. "I am not jealous of these... these monsters! These misfits!" Francesa grabbed a book and flung it at me. It hit the wall where my leg should be, but the dirt absorbed the impact. "I use magic for good!"

"Is that why you killed three people and strung them up behind City Hall?"

The crazy woman laughed. "They were only the beginning."

It All Comes Down

My husband was trapped half in, half out of a wall of mud and dirt while a crazy woman talked at him, and I had no idea how to free him.

"Can we dig him out?" Angel asked, while I stared at Dan through a crack in the door and chewed my lower lip. "Maybe it's just that simple."

"Maybe it is, but Francesca is right there." I peeked into the room, where she continued pacing and waving her hands around while she performed her evil villain monologue for poor trapped Dan. "Although she doesn't appear to be all together."

"However you decide to move forward, you two must stay close to each other," Jacob said. "This house is imbued with magic. When Alex broke the perimeter ward, I suspect he also weakened the structure."

"Are you saying the house is going to fall on us?" I demanded, then I shook my head. "Don't answer that. Angel, grab a weapon. We're getting Dan, then we're getting out."

Angel grabbed a glass beaker and a length of tubing, then she adjusted something in her coat pocket. "Let's go."

I took a breath, then I opened the door and strode into the room. The smell of rot hit me in the face, and I almost retched again. "Disgusting," I muttered, then Francesca saw us and halted.

"Hey," I said with a wave. "Nice to see you again. You really like being underground, huh?"

"Below is safe," Francesca hissed. "No witches are down in the dirt."

"And yet you're down here stealing witch powers." I sent a tendril of magic toward Dan. I saw his brow pinch, then chunks of the dirt wall started falling to the floor, which was good. My intent had been to dry out the mud, so Dan could pull himself loose. Now I just had to keep Francesca talking until he was free. "What was with you putting on Cecily Allwood's face?"

"That bitch," Francesca said in a high-pitched squeal. "She swayed my brother! She convinced him that he should leave me for her!"

I sucked in a breath, and decided to ignore the darker implications of that statement. "Is that why you killed him?"

"I was trying to help him," Francesca snarled. "I tried to purge the witch stain from him, but it was too deep."

"Is that what you did to Jerry Goldman?" I pressed. "What about Colleen? Were they tainted, too?"

"They all deserved their fates," Francesca screamed, then Jared Besami rolled out of his chair and onto the floor. Before I could figure out if he was alive or a corpse, Dan pulled himself out of the wall and grabbed Francesca in a chokehold.

"It's over, Francesca," Dan said, as she clawed at his arm. "We're all gonna leave now, nice and calm, and we're gonna get you some help."

"I don't need help," she shrieked, then a metal canister dropped into her hand and she sprayed Dan in the face. His grip weakened enough for her to slip free, and she ran toward the lab room.

"Enjoy your time beneath," she said, then the ceiling came down on top of us.

Digging Out

When the house started falling, I didn't have time to think. My eyes were burning and I couldn't see, thanks to the mace, but I could hear people talking. I flung myself toward Eli's voice and grabbed her as clods of dirt and rocks began crashing to the floor. Terrified for her and the baby, I covered her body with my own.

"Get out of here," I said, as tears streamed down my face. Only some were from the mace. "Use magic! Go! Don't worry about me."

"Dan, no." I felt Eli's hands on my face, and the sting lessened. I never knew she could heal with a touch. "I'm not leaving you."

"Think of the baby." I could deal with me getting flattened under a crazy woman's house, but Eli and our baby needed to live. As I braced myself for impact, I realized one wasn't happening. The house had... stopped falling?

The pain in my eyes lessened to that of a mild sunburn, and I cracked one open. Amazingly, we weren't buried alive. Also, Angel, Jacob, and LeClerc were sitting on the ground next to us, also not buried.

"What," I began, then I looked up. Dirt and debris formed a perfectly smooth dome over our head, and we were safe inside a pocket of air. "Protection bubble?"

"With a little power boost from Jacob and LeClerc," Eli said, then she fit herself against me. "You okay?"

I kissed her hair. "Never better, baby." I glanced at Angel. "How are you holding up?"

"Peachy," she replied. "And I've got the best present for my Jilly." With a grin, Angel pulled out her phone and a notebook. "I recorded that nut job's confession, and I've got her list of people she's taken body parts from. Now you'll have evidence you can use in the real world, not only at a witch tribunal or whatever it is you do."

"I haven't been to a tribunal in over a hundred years," Jacob said. "They were much more common in the Old Country."

"You're forgetting the tribunal held in the autumn of sixty-eight," LeClerc said. "It concerned the use of music as an enthrallment device."

"Ah, yes," Jacob said. "You've always had the better memory."

"Hey, Angel," I said. "Give Jill a call so they can start digging us out."

Angel put her phone to her ear. "On it."

WHAT?

It took hours for the rescue squad to dig us out. So, that was boring but she used them to maintain her party girl lifestyle. After Megan entered the picture, and she started hanging out with Lillian, they brought Jerry Goldman into the fold—but all he wanted was money. When things got desperate, Lillian floated the idea of ransoming Abby.

"She must have ice in her veins," I muttered, when LeClerc revealed that detail. "How could someone put up their own niece like that?"

"My mother says some people are born wicked," Angel said. "But the baby girl is safe, and her nasty aunt won't be hurting her any more."

Jacob materialized next to LeClerc. He sat next to him on the dirt floor and took his hand. "Francesca has been located, still raving like a lunatic," he told us. "I eavesdropped on what was happening, and according to Megan, the three deaths that started this case were an accident; in fact, it was Francesca's killing of them that led to her going to Nine Lives Investigations in order to create an alibi for herself. And it was Lillian's idea to string the victims up behind City

Hall. Her reasoning was if people were scared of the government, fewer people would vote for the incumbent mayor, thus helping her own campaign."

"She has no morals and no common sense," Dan declared. "Staging a witch hunt won't affect the election one way or the other."

"At least she won't be mayor," I said, and we all nodded. "What are they going to do with Francesca?"

"For now, she's being transported to a psychiatric facility," Jacob replied. "While I do believe she must atone for her crimes, what she really needs is medical attention."

"No argument there," Angel said. "As long as she's not at my hospital."

I leaned into Dan's side. He put his arm around me, and kissed my hair. "Yeah, she needs to be sent someplace like Bellevue," I began, then the ground shook and a huge chunk of the dirt over our heads was whisked away. After my eyes adjusted to the light, I saw Tessa standing on the edge of what used to be the basement.

"Hello, everyone," she called, as she dusted off her hands. "I would have been here sooner, but it's hard to magically shift an entire house without anyone noticing. Want to get out of here?"

I missed my obstetrics appointment on Monday morning.

It wasn't my fault I overslept, what with everything that happened to us over the weekend. Okay, maybe it was a little my fault, since I deliberately turned off all of our alarms the day before. Whatever, we needed the sleep.

Dan was mortified. When he called the office to reschedule our appointment, he must have apologized a dozen times.

"I'm sure people miss appointments all the time," I said, when he hung up. We were in the kitchen, and I was having my gourmet breakfast of dry toast and black coffee. "It's not a big deal."

"You're right." He plunked a kiss on my forehead as he walked past me to the coffee machine. "And we've got an appointment for three."

"Really?" I whined. "I wanted this to be a pajama day."

"Wear pajamas to the doctor, if you want." Dan sat across from me, and took my hand. "Listen, after everything that happened, we need to make sure both of you are okay. That's why we need this appointment. And don't give me that protection bubble spiel," he said, when I began protesting. "I humor you about a lot of shit. You can humor me, just this once, and go to this appointment."

He began rubbing his thumb across my knuckles. My eyes narrowed, because he knew I liked that. My husband was playing dirty. "Fine. But we're having pajama day tomorrow and you're making me pancakes."

Dan kissed my knuckles. "Whatever you want, baby."

Despite all my complaining, the obstetrics appointment wasn't so bad. Everyone in the office was super nice, and the doctor was kind and patient with Dan's thousand questions, but the icing on the cake was at the end of the visit and we had our second ultrasound.

"There he is," I said, when the screen showed us the black and gray swirls that made me choke up with happy tears. "He's good?"

"They are," the doctor replied. "Hang on, I'll turn on the volume so you can hear the heartbeats."

"Wait," Dan said. "Heartbeats? As in, plural?"

"Yes," the doctor said, as she turned a knob and the sound of two rapid heartbeats filled the examination room. "You're having twins."

I stared from the screen, to the smiling doctor, to Dan's utterly bewildered face. "What?"

I hope you enjoyed Eli and Dan's latest adventure. The next installment, **Holly and Ivy**, will be available in 2026.

If you're new to the series and wondering how these supernatural hijinks all began, check out Eli's first case in Belladonna, available wherever books are sold.

Happy reading!

Also By Jennifer Allis Provost

The Order of the Phoenix

The Phoenix and the Cat

Phoenix Rising

Dragon Descending

The Chronicles of Parthalan, a six volume epic fantasy (and one short story collection)

Heir to the Sun

The Virgin Queen

Rise of the Deva'shi

Pieces of Parthalan: Six All-New Stories From The Land of Parthalan

Golem

Elfsong

Sunfall

The Copper Legacy, a four book urban fantasy:

Copper Girl

Copper Ravens

Copper Veins

Copper Princess

A duology based in the Copper world:

Redemption

Salvation

Poison Garden, an urban fantasy filled with seers, witches, and one seriously hot detective:

Belladonna

Oleander

Bleeding Hearts

Thornapple

Wolfsbane

Mistletoe

Mandrake

Holly and Ivy

Gallowglass, an urban fantasy set in Scotland and New York:

Gallowglass

Walker

Homecoming

The Shades of Elphame

Winter's Queen, an urban fantasy set in Scotland and Elphame:

Touch of Frost

Giant's Daughter

Elphame's Queen

Merrowkin, an urban fantasy set in Ireland above and below

A Sea of Secrets and Salvation

Merrowkin

Death's Door

Manannán's Pearl

Changes, a contemporary romance:

Changing Teams

Changing Scenes

Changing Fate

Changing Dates

About The Author

Jennifer Allis Provost is a native New Englander who lives in a sprawling colonial along with her beautiful and precocious twins, a dog that thinks she's a kangaroo, a parrot, a junkyard cat, and a wonderful husband who never forgets to buy ice cream. As a child, she read anything and everything she could get her hands on, including a set of encyclopedias, but fantasy was always her favorite. She spends her days drinking vast amounts of coffee, arguing with her computer, and avoiding any and all domestic behavior.

Find Jenn on the web here: http://authorjenniferallisprovost.com/

For up to the minute sale notifications, follow her on Bookbub here: https://www.bookbub.com/profile/jennifer-allis-provost

For exclusive content, follow her on Patreon: https://www.patreon.com/jenniferallisprovost/

Friend her on Facebook: http://www.facebook.com/jennallis

Follow her on Instagram: @jenniferaprovost

Happy reading!